About the Author

Hazel Smith had an overwhelming ambition to become an author from a young age. For years she wrote short stories but was too afraid to seek publication. On her retirement, Hazel enrolled in a creative writing course, which rekindled her passion for writing and gave her a new desire to write novels. This is the author's second book, and she intends to continue writing as long as she can and has something worthwhile to say.

Verna Earl and the Rich Lady

Hazel Smith

Verna Earl and the Rich Lady

Olympia Publishers
London

www.olympiapublishers.com
OLYMPIA PAPERBACK EDITION

Copyright © Hazel Smith 2025

The right of Hazel Smith to be identified as author of this work has been asserted in accordance with sections 77 and 78 of the Copyright, Designs and Patents Act 1988.

All Rights Reserved

No reproduction, copy or transmission of this publication may be made without written permission. No paragraph of this publication may be reproduced, copied or transmitted save with the written permission of the publisher, or in accordance with the provisions of the Copyright Act 1956 (as amended).

Any person who commits any unauthorised act in relation to this publication may be liable to criminal prosecution and civil claims for damage.

A CIP catalogue record for this title is available from the British Library.

ISBN: 978-1-83543-251-8

This is a work of fiction.
Names, characters, places and incidents originate from the writer's imagination. Any resemblance to actual persons, living or dead, is purely coincidental.

First Published in 2025

Olympia Publishers
Tallis House
2 Tallis Street
London
EC4Y 0AB

Printed in Great Britain

Dedication

I dedicate this book to my daughter, Chrissy.

Acknowledgements

Thanks to my son, Keith, for his encouragement and help with editing.

Chapter 1

Beginnings

Earl's Journey

For years Earl and his mother shared a shack, and when she died suddenly before she reached her fortieth, he, just twelve years old, found himself alone in the world. There were no other relatives to look after the boy; they were either all dead or had abandoned the little isle in the Caribbean Sea for larger islands somewhere. They used to live away from the tiny township settlement on the tiny Grenadine island of Mayron, a chain of small islands lying south of the much larger main island, St Vincent, in the West Indies.

Earl's mother, Rosanna Drake, was called 'odd' and 'crazy' by almost all their compatriots, and although no one said it openly, some felt sorry for her little boy being dragged around the island on a daily basis. After her death, he continued to wander around the island aimlessly, lonely, friendless and longing to escape.

He dreamt of the day that he would be able to build a sturdy house on the very spot where the shack stood – his home since birth. Unfortunately, a few days after his mother's death, their ramshackle abode fell down, an omen people said. He was sensitive to the murmurings and decided to leave Mayron as soon as he could save up for a one-way ticket to the main island. His mother's only friend Rhoda helped, but he was starving and wanted to make something of himself; he had to go where he could at least find work. Any work would do, as there was nothing at all on tiny Mayron for a young man to do, except maybe fishing. He didn't want to do that; he wasn't a lover of the unpredictable sea, though he saw it every day of his waking life. He hoped his decision to relocate would put money in his pocket and food in his belly.

Years later, in 1950, and just after he turned seventeen, the day came when he was able to leave Mayron. He swore never to return to the small, beautiful island and the daily pain he had endured there. On the bay front to see him off were the only friends he and Rosanna ever had, Rhoda Simons and her young daughter, Verna.

"Come back soon," said Rhoda as she and little Verna waved him off.

He smiled and jumped on board the small sailing boat that would take him northwards to St Vincent. Once, as a small child, he and his mother went there briefly, apparently for her to see a 'head' doctor, so people said. But she didn't like the isolated hospital she was sent to, which was tucked away within the forest well inland from civilisation and which she said was full of 'crazy' people. Although she was a patient there, she managed to escape, collected her child from the minder who was looking after him, and then somehow acquired passage back home to Mayron. She swore never to set foot on St Vincent's soil again because some ignorant people in Kingstown laughed at her and called her names. Little Earl only saw the town as huge, bewildering and full of people.

Ah, come back when ah rich, he thought to himself as he sat low down in the boat, looking back at the only two friends he had in the world standing on the hot silver sand, waving him goodbye. Young Verna, just ten years old, and her mother watched as the boat turned, the one large sail unfurled, and the breeze pushed the tiny yacht out into the Caribbean Sea. As the boat sailed around the headland and out of sight, Verna and her mother were the only people left on the beach.

Walking home, Rhoda prayed silently that the young man and indeed the whole boat complement would arrive safely at Kingstown, the capital. The voyage northwards could be fraught with menace, the sea could be deceptively flat and glass-like, the breeze low and steady when the little yacht weighed anchor. However, before it reached the isle of Bequia, twenty miles or so to the north and nine miles south of the main island, a wild wind could replace the gentle breeze, and the flat, glass-like, shiny surface of the sea could become rough and mountainous. Many boats – small and large – had been lost to the sea, many lives cut short, so Rhoda's prayers were earnest and profound.

Three days later, the ferry boat returned to Mayron. Rhoda was greatly relieved, and she thanked God for Earl's safe entrance on the main island. She was glad he was where he wanted to be but sad that she may never see him again. Kingstown, in the 1950s, was small but growing fast, and she hoped Earl would get a job and improve himself as his heart desired in time.

Verna and Bequia

The years passed, and Verna grew tall, slim and beautiful in her smooth, light-brown skin. She and her mother never heard from Earl again, not even at Christmas, when Rhoda had hoped he would send them a card with maybe a dollar or two enclosed. Rhoda wished she knew where he was staying so she could send him news of what was happening in their little far-off world.

"Ma, I have to go away to find work; there's nothing here for me to do," said Verna on the day she turned fifteen and some five years after Earl had left Mayron.

Rhoda feared the day would come when she had to see her child leave home to find work. What would happen to a single young woman in Kingstown or anywhere else for that matter, she pondered. There must be something she could do or someone in their community willing to oblige.

"I'll ask Mrs Lamour. She'd help!" said Rhoda hopefully.

"No, Ma, there's nothing here; not even Mrs Lamour can take on more servants."

Verna was right; Mrs Lamour, store and fishing boat owner, was the richest person on the island and the largest employer, and they both knew that many of the grown-up islanders were already employed by her.

"I know that. I'll leave, and you can have my job. I'll get by." Rhoda was desperate to keep her child close to her.

"Ma, there's plenty of work on the main island. Plenty of rich people over there; I surely can find work of some sort!" She didn't really know that but had heard people say so.

Rhoda knew her daughter was right, and though she didn't want her only child to leave home and move so far away overseas, she knew it was the only solution. Verna was smart and did well at the small school she had been a regular at until she turned thirteen. She had excelled at reading, writing and arithmetic but on Mayron, that was as far as she could go; with no secondary schools there. She would have to go to St Vincent for that privilege, and it was expensive. Rhoda was resigned to the coming separation.

Several months later, and after a struggle for Verna to find work of any kind in her homeland, like Earl had done before, the ladies sailed northwards. They were not going to the main island, as Verna preferred, but to Bequia, which was a little nearer to Mayron and which Rhoda had begged her daughter to try first to find employment. Rhoda hoped Verna would find a job in Bequia, but if she was not successful, then they would move on further north to St Vincent. They were only going to stay one day, walking to the few big houses and all the businesses asking and hoping. By the time they boarded the sailboat later that day to sail back home, Verna was employed. She was going to work for Mr and Mrs Cassocks, rich business people, owners of land, fishing, boat builders and stores.

"Well, you leave me for good now," said Rhoda despondently as they arrived back home.

"No, Ma, I'm only going to work there, every month I'd send money back home." Verna was upbeat and was behaving as though she had bagged a top job.

"I know, my darling daughter, but I'll still miss you." She was full of worries that her teenage daughter was forced to move so far away for work; it was times like this that she wished they didn't live on such a tiny island.

Verna had big ideas and had never intended to be a maid, but her education was not up to getting a better job, and she knew she had to strive harder to achieve more. One day, she imagined, she'd be working somewhere smart and making good money. A week later, Rhoda held her daughter tightly in her arms and cried copiously, begging her to stay but encouraging her to go moments before she boarded the ferry boat to sail northwards. Verna wished her mother would stop the caterwauling and promised her she'd be just fine, but Rhoda was inconsolable.

Later that day, Verna stepped off the ferry then made her way to the imposing house on the hill overlooking Port Elizabeth, Bequia's main town and port. Her bravado gone; she was shaking like a leaf as she walked through Port Elizabeth towards her new workplace. She quickly arrived at the large Colonial-style dazzling white house, which sported the customary wide veranda almost encircling the house. A boy about her age dressed in a ragged shirt with most of the buttons missing and worn khaki shorts, stopped weeding and stared open-mouthed at the newcomer.

"You catch fly," she addressed him, feigning confidence, "I'm expected."

"So, yuh, dat new girl expected!" He smiled and licked his lips while his eyes moved up and down Verna's half-girl, half-woman body.

"Just show me the way to go, fresh boy!"

He pointed the way up the path round the back of the house, then hopped in front of her to personally show her where to go. By the side of the house, the boy called out by the half door.

"Miss Bernice, dat new girl come!"

He turned to continue ogling Verna when Miss Bernice appeared at the door.

"Go way, boy, go do yuh wok. Leave dis girl alone. Yuh hear?"

"Yes, Miss," He dropped his cocky head and scurried off.

"Come, chile," she said and welcomed Verna with a smile and warm embrace.

The boy had compounded her fear of being so far away from her mother, but Miss Bernice's warmth melted her. She began to take heed of her mother's advice: be aware of what's going on around, beware of men and empty promises, do your job well, and tackle each day as it presents itself.

She opened her mouth in awe; she had never seen inside a rich person's home before, and she was amazed at the size of the kitchen.

My goodness, this one room is bigger than our little house. Some people are born with silver spoons in their mouths!

"Is this where I'm going to work, in this big room, Miss Bernice?" she asked, bewildered.

Miss Bernice threw her head back and burst into a loud, crude laugh. "No, yuh don't wok hay, yuh de housemaid, not cook!"

Verna was told that she would work in the rest of the house but never in the kitchen. She was taken back outside and into a side door to a room that she would share with another maid. She tested the narrow bed with its wired base and thin horsehair mattress, placed her grip under it, and cried. Her bravery had evaporated; she missed Rhoda tremendously; she had never been away from her mother before, and she felt like a small abandoned child.

The next day her roommate woke her up at six a.m. and handed her a couple of white full aprons and a little white stiffly starched hat that looked very much like a nurse's. After their breakfast, which they collected from the kitchen, they entered the house by another back door into a room full of dried washing, brooms, dust-cloths and more paraphernalia than anything she had ever seen or imagined. Verna's new roommate was the no-nonsense but a little jaded, older, shrewder Elisha, who would roll her eyes and suck her teeth to empathise with her disgust with the monotonous work they undertook daily. She proceeded to instruct Verna about her duties and how she should carry them out.

Starting with wiping her sandalled feet properly before entering the house, keeping the aprons and hat, which would sit perched on her head and held in place with hairpins, scrupulously clean, and making sure she never entered a room when a family member was present.

They would make beds with clean sheets and pillowcases every day, dust, polish, sweep the wooden floors and mop. Then there would be mountains of ironing to do on laundry days, but thankfully another woman, Dorcas, came on those days to wash the clothes. Elisha ignored the fact that she was lucky to have a job and her dirt-poor family on Canouan, another Grenadine island, benefitted from the tedious and boring work she hated but had to do. Verna was pleased that the older women she worked with, the estate manager, Mr Vernon, who had employed her, and even the many young men working outdoors treated her with respect. Miss Bernice hovered like a mother hen over her sometimes, which she found tedious, but she was respectful of the older woman's caring attitude towards her.

She had seen the master and mistress briefly a few times a good way off and was warned by the other staff to never cross the couple's path and keep well out of sight. All the housework should be done by the time the couple returns home for lunch. She and Elisha spent a great deal of time in the utility room, where she helped with sorting, ironing and folding a never-ending mountain of household laundry. While they did their chores, they would talk of the family and friends they left behind on the other islands. Verna was a little saddened that Elisha's family of three children and a sickly husband who was unable to work were back on Canouan. This Grenadine island was smaller than Bequia but considerably larger than Mayron and lay in the chain south of Bequia but north of Mayron.

"Must be hard leaving little children behind. I don't think I could do that," said Verna, admiring Elisha's fortitude.

"Yes, hard, but I had no choice. Mamie looks after them and Wilbur, my sick husband."

"How old are your children, Elisha?"

"Micky twelve, he's big like me now, Sondra ten, little Percy eight. They don't miss me cause they know when I come home I bring a big trunk of stuff..." She trailed off as the pain of being away from her children dug into her. "...come on, let's get this done," she said with a little tremble in her voice.

Verna settled in well, and to her embarrassment, she sometimes forgot her mother was home alone back on Mayron. A tear would roll down her cheek as sadness replaced her complacency, she hoped Rhoda was coping well without her.

One day, much more relaxed in her new environment, Verna was rubbing the mahogany dining table with an energy that could burnish the shine. She was startled by a voice behind her.

"Any harder, and you'll rub off the varnish. That would be unfortunate!"

She spun around to face Mrs Cassocks and found herself sputtering incoherently. She dropped her head and eyes and tried to speak; she never thought the mistress would still be at home; otherwise, she would never have entered the house with such nonchalance.

"What's your name, girl?" Mrs Cassocks asked the visibly shaking girl in front of her.

"Verna, Mrs Cassocks," she spluttered.

"You, local?"

"No, Miss, I'm from Mayron."

"Lovely little place; I went there once; too small for human habitation, I think. A big Atlantic wave during a hurricane could easily swamp it. Never mind, so you're the new maid?"

She didn't give Verna time to answer; she walked away towards the veranda and was soon out of sight. Verna picked up the dusters and walked hurriedly to the utility where Elisha was ironing.

"Oh, my God, Mistress Cassocks came into the dining room while I was polishing the table. I nearly dropped dead!" She sat down heavily on the nearest chair.

Elisha looked gloomy and said deadpan, "She will sack you now; they don't like servants around them, unless they call you!"

"But I didn't know she was home," said Verna, alarmed.

"That's no excuse; you make sure nobody is around before you go into a room. Ah, told you so before!" said Elisha with the accusing tone one assumes when talking to a wayward child.

Verna waited thereafter to be sacked, and every day she made sure she peeked around the door before entering a room. The shock came suddenly one afternoon several weeks later. Bernice ordered her to go to the mistress who was lounging on the veranda.

"Well, I guess that's it; I'm out of a job," she said weakly.

"Girl," said Bernice impatiently, "just go and stop wishing yourself bad."

Verna stood in front of the reclining Mrs Cassocks, who appeared to be asleep on the low, locally made lounger on the wide veranda with its smooth, dark wooden flooring, facing the white ornate spindles held in place with a solid black balustrade. She noted the lady wasn't very old, in fact younger than her mother, with dead straight blond hair falling loosely down onto her shoulders. She was slim, well-toned and sported the most beautiful manicured nails Verna had ever seen on any woman's fingers.

"Excuse me, Mrs Cassocks; Miss Bernice said you want me," she said to the reclining lady.

"Did you go to school, Verna?" Mrs Cassocks sounded warm and friendlier than before but didn't even turn her head to look at the frightened girl.

"Yes, Mrs Cassocks," replied Verna, a little confused.

"Up to secondary school?" she asked the girl unnecessarily. After all, an educated girl would never be satisfied with low-paid work such as servant work.

"No, Miss, Ma couldn't afford to send me to high school in Kingstown, and I didn't get a scholarship. But I stayed in school until I reached thirteen." Verna always felt ashamed of her lack of further education and dreamt of achieving that goal one day.

"So how old are you now?"

"Nearly sixteen, Miss."

"Do you like to read?" she asked, being aware that poor people didn't have the money to buy books but knew libraries were available even in a tiny country. "We've got hundreds of books, and hardly anyone reads them."

Verna knew that. She had dusted the many shelves from floor to ceiling creaking with books of all kinds; some were large tomes of which she needed her two hands while wiping the dust off. She often wished she could take one of the thinner books with her to read in her room or while she sat under the Grafted Mango tree in her spare time. Perhaps rich people just filled their homes with things they don't need because it made them look important and smart. She was puzzled by the lady's line of questioning but said she loved reading and had read most of the Bible plus books from the small library on Mayron and any other material that came her way.

"Then you can read to me. Go and pick a book, any one, then come and read it aloud to me."

Verna was stunned. Just before she turned to fetch a book, she glanced again at her employer and wondered why a woman as young as her, possibly around thirty years old, couldn't read for herself. However, Verna's first impression of this white woman filled her with a warm feeling she couldn't comprehend at all. While she dusted the numerous shelves of books, she had noted the titles and authors of some of the books, many of whom she had never heard of. However, she went straight to a shelf nearest the door, closed her eyes and picked a book. It happened to be a book called 'Jane Eyre' by Charlotte Brontë.

"I got one, Miss!" she said with a girlish glee, holding the leather-clad book aloft.

"Ahh, a Bronte sister," Mrs Cassocks said when Verna held the book in front of her face. "They were three sisters who lived in England a long time ago." She looked up at Verna, whose eyes were sparkling. She smiled and asked mischievously, already knowing the answer. "Have you heard of the Brontes?"

"No, Miss, but I heard of another English author called Charles Dickens, and I read a couple of his books. I really enjoyed the one called 'Oliver Twist.'

"Well, good for you! I'm not too keen on him, but I love the Brontes. I love Charlotte; her work's full of passion. Sit down and read to me." She smiled and closed her eyes, relaxing herself on her luxurious daybed, the chaise lounge.

"Yes, Miss." Verna was pleased she had unwittingly picked a book her mistress particularly loved. She held the book as though it was a precious jewel, carefully examined the cover, ran her fingers around the edges, and then, catching herself, opened to the first chapter.

She began to read slowly and tentatively at first but soon got into the flow, unaware that she was reading with a quiet passion; she completely forgot she had an audience.

"My, you're good! Let's leave it there till next time," said the grateful listener.

Verna reluctantly closed the book and looked across at her reclining mistress. As she stood up to leave, Mrs Cassocks said, "Tomorrow, same time."

"Yes, Mrs Cassocks. Goodnight!"

"Goodnight," replied the recumbent lady who wanted to say 'sleep tight' to this lovely brown-skinned girl.

She wanted to ask Verna to stay and chat, to have a twilight stroll with her. She was lonely and longed for new friends to fill the empty days of doing nothing more than sit in the sailing club house or the country club listening to boring talk uttered by spoilt, privileged women. She longed for new adventures with people closer to her age and often fantasised hooking arms with beautiful black girls she saw round and about; she longed to share their adventures.

Verna's life was changing; she was becoming well read and more articulate, and with her almost daily interactions with the mistress, she was being transformed into a maturity she could never have dreamt of before. A few months later, she returned home to Mayron for a week's break. Rhoda immediately saw the change in her daughter; her speech had become less vernacular, and there was a new sophistication in her bearing that made her mother feel a little like a poor, uneducated relative.

She was amazed when Verna looked over their meagre home with a critical eye and made galling remarks about the poverty of the place. She was staggered that the girl had already forgotten where she came from after being away for such a short time and being nothing more but the paid home help. Verna had longed to return home to see her mother and to enjoy the land of her birth and her friends. But Bequia and Mrs Cassocks had changed her view of the world; she was dismayed that a whole week would be wasted on Mayron. However, seeing her mother's sad face shook her up and brought her back to reality.

"Ma, why don't you come to live in Bequia?" she ventured one late afternoon while they sat in front of their tiny home watching the sun go down in the dark blue Caribbean Sea.

"What, leave my home, my friends, my people in the graveyard?" Rhoda was angry. How dare this girl be so flippant with her feelings?

"Don't fuss, Ma; I just think it would be better with us together. And no sea to cross. I don't like those little sailing boats." Her voice was gentle; she didn't want to upset her mother any more, but she did see Bequia as a better prospect with more opportunities than the tiny, sparsely populated Mayron.

"I ain't going nowhere; I'll never leave my home. Never!" She stomped off down to the deserted beach just a few yards away.

Verna felt the tremor of her mother's anger and ran after her to make amends.

"Ma, sorry for upsetting you, but I promise you that one day I'd get a better-paid job and I'd send more money for you to repair the house and improve our standard of living."

After Verna returned to her work, she made a decision that she was going to ask her friendly mistress how she could improve her life. She didn't want to be a maid forever; she had her heart set on an office job or perhaps a job in a fancy store.

"You're going to ask, what?" screamed Elisha as they lay on their respective narrow beds one night, waiting for sleep. "You crazy! She kicks your ass outta here if you ask for a better job."

"All I'm going to ask for is a job in her store." Verna saw no harm in asking, after all, the mistress was kind, friendly and encouraging, but Elisha's doubts were worrying.

"Verna, you're a servant girl; mistress won't appreciate you asking for work improvement. Listen to me, girl, don't be fooled by her friendliness; if you bother her, she will sack you just like that." Elisha clicked her fingers for emphasis, which resonated through the darkened room.

Verna appeased Elisha by promising to keep her thoughts of improvement to herself, but she still couldn't see why asking her rich mistress for advice would jeopardise her current situation. She was summoned as usual to read, but that day she wasn't in the mood and went begrudgingly to do her task. She couldn't refuse; she had no choice but to do her mistress' bidding.

She joined Mrs Cassocks on the veranda with the book they half read last time, 'Jane Austen's Sense and Sensibility.' Unsmiling, she politely greeted the rich lady, sat down and began to read vacuously.

Something wasn't right. The girl had lost her spark and was reading in a flat droll without the usual passion. Mrs Cassocks felt betrayed that her kindness was being thrown back in her face. She stopped the session.

"That's enough today. Off you go!"

"Yes, miss," said Verna in a low, bored voice, then scurried off.

"Yuh, back quick!" said the ever-observant Elisha.

"Huh, she's anxious about something; sent me away after only a few pages." Verna had completely misread the situation – that her behaviour may have affected her mistress's mood.

"See, you ask for something, you get sacked!"

"No, I didn't ask her for anything. Not sure why she's so unhappy today."

They both surmised it must be husband trouble that soured Mrs Cassocks mood and decided to put the incident behind them. But Verna at last could see it would be folly to ask for anything, and she began to despair. She was surely trapped forever doing housework for others. Tears welled up at the realisation that she would die in poverty just like her grandparents and the continuing penury of her mother.

The mistress didn't ask her to read for some time, and one day, just as she finished dusting the hanging pictures on the living-room wooden walls, a movement caught her eye; she turned to see Mrs Cassocks walking towards the veranda. She sneaked closer to have a peek to see what the silent lady was up to and got a shock. She rushed outside in tears to where Elisha was helping Dorcas, the washerwoman, hang laundry on the clothesline.

"What's wrong, girlie?" Elisha asked, putting an arm around the sobbing Verna.

"She's done with me. She's reading for herself now. I don't think she likes me any more." Her whole body rocked with sadness and abandonment.

"Look girl, Ah did tell you don't have high hopes because she took a shine to you. She's lazy, just like all the rich people like her; she could read for herself, but she only wants to keep yuh busy when you've done the housework."

At last Verna understood; all the friendliness her employer showed her was an illusion; she had stupidly thought she cared. She had misread the smiles, the warm looks, the gentle voice, and now she felt a proper fool. From now on, she decided she'd be what God intended her to be, a lowly servant seeing to other people's needs.

As the weeks passed, Verna still hoped and prayed she would bag a better job. Whenever she walked along the main road down in Port Elizabeth and seeing what she thought were other fulfilling job opportunities, she contrived ways she could ask for a job without arousing suspicion with her employers.

Sometimes she would casually ask in small shops and stores, in a jokey manner, if jobs were available. When asked if she was looking for work, she would quickly reply that she was enquiring for a friend because she already had a job. She had to be smart because if word got back to Mrs Cassocks, she surely would be sacked for disloyalty and would end up with no job at all.

During her many wanderings around Port Elizabeth on her days off, she eventually made friends with a couple of girls her age, Muriel and Lorna. The girls, who weren't related, lived in the poor, rundown neighbourhood of scattered houses on the other side of Port Elizabeth, and like her, they wished every day to escape.

Muriel, who helped out part time in the creche for poor working mothers where her mother worked, dreamt of living abroad somewhere, toying with the idea of moving to England permanently. Lorna sat wistfully five days a week in a small tumbledown shop near her home, selling home-made food and bread for old Mr Martin and his sick wife.

The three young women would sit on the hot, glistening silver sands on Lower Bay Beach, then soak themselves in the calm, salty sea for ages, chatting and hoping for better days. Young men were usually interested, looking, ogling and sometimes being downright fresh with the girls. If it got too much, especially when they annoyingly swam around the three friends in the sea, got too close and salacious, spoiling the girls' day, they would leave the beach and go home. None of the girls wanted to be bogged down at such a young age with men or children; they were ambitious, and life was lamentably limited for them on Bequia.

Lorna was the first to leave; she was going to train to become a qualified nurse on the main island. Verna was jealous; she really wanted to go as well but didn't want to become a nurse. She could be a nurse's aid at first, as Lorna would be doing before she took an academic test to see if she would be good enough to train to become a registered nurse. Despite encouragement from Lorna, Verna didn't want to go near a hospital. Not long after Lorna left Bequia, Muriel followed.

Verna cried continually that night out of sadness over losing her only friends and of longing to better herself but not sure what she wanted to do or what she could actually do to improve herself. Sometimes, while cleaning the veranda, which continued around the western side of the house and was wide enough for all the chairs, loungers and even a dining table just in case the home owners fancied eating 'outside' for a change, she would stop to ponder. She would have swept its dark wooden floor and thoroughly dusted all its ornate spindles and the long, robust handrail. She would be struggling with longing and loneliness while looking down on the roofs of Port Elizabeth, the small boats and yachts bobbing about in its calm harbour, and the empty beauty of Lower Bay.

"Go do nursing like Lorna if you are so sad missing her." Elisha was a little bored of her continual harping about a better life but doing nothing about it like her friends did.

"No, I don't want to do nursing, but I do want better than this!" She made a flourish with her arm to emphasise the point. Then realising she was talking to someone who was stuck forever with her lot as a servant, she apologised to Elisha that she wasn't looking down on her or servant work.

Elisha wasn't upset; she understood and hoped the girl, close to eighteen years of age, got her wish to do something a bit better than servant work. She decided to ask around to help her move on, but things took an unexpected turn a few days later.

Bernice hurried to the utility room, where Elisha was ironing and Verna was sorting and folding laundry. She told Verna Mrs Cassocks wanted her on the veranda right away.

"Who me?" asked the bewildered girl, pointing to herself.

She had not seen the mistress for ages since she stopped reading for her and had forgotten all about her except that she was employed by her and living under her roof.

"Yes, go; don't keep her waiting," said the jittery Bernice.

Verna stood in front of Mrs Cassocks, who was on the chaise lounge, as usual. Her eyes were closed, the back of one hand resting casually on her forehead and the other resting on her flat abdomen. Verna wasn't sure what to say, so she remained standing, still and quietly.

"Sit down, Verna," said the lady without moving an inch.

Verna did as she was commanded and pulled up one of the strange half metal, half plastic chairs around and sat down facing her mistress. A few minutes of quiet were alarming her, and her heart was beating a little too fast. She was finding it difficult to keep still; her legs began twitching.

"How are you keeping? Happy?" The lady stirred, moving her head to the side to look at the girl.

"Ah, I'm OK, Miss. Happy!" She was lying, but what can she say? She didn't want to upset her mistress again.

"I called you because I want you to read again." Then, after a pause while she looked over at the girl, she quietly added, "I missed you!"

This was a monumental shock to Verna. She missed me? I thought she was mad at me. She ignored me for weeks! She realised how naïve she was because she had been unable to understand the nuances of a fellow human's behaviour.

In spite of herself, she smiled warmly, and their eyes sparkled with mutual respect. She was instructed to fetch a book, any one to her liking, and start reading when she was ready. Verna was full of passion again, and, unaware of her behaviour, she gesticulated to emphasise the more dramatic passages of the book as she read. It was a while before she caught herself and glanced up from the book to see a smiling Mrs Cassocks on her side facing her, completely enthralled. Her words tailed off.

"Oh, don't stop." Arlene Cassocks spun herself round and sat up, then said, "No. Please leave it there; you must be tired."

Verna wanted to say she wasn't tired and that she wanted to continue; she was enjoying the book immensely, but she pulled back, not wanting to appear presumptuous.

"Come back tomorrow, same time. Oh, when you come to read again, don't wear your uniform." She stood up and followed Verna into the library, and as they parted, she touched the girl's arm. Verna nearly fainted.

She couldn't understand her mistress's sudden turn around and how, after weeks of uncertainty, of hardly seeing her and sometimes not sure if she was at home at all, Verna decided in a very grown-up way to take each day as it comes and never hope for more. Elisha was pleased the girl was in Mrs Cassocks' favour again but warned her to stay focused and do her job well. She decided she won't bother to look for or ask for a better job; there wasn't anything to choose from anyway, and worse, she wasn't educated enough to elevate herself. She began to live for those reading sessions; she could temporarily forget she was a maid and catapult herself into another world of intrigue and adventure where she didn't have to dust, sweep, polish, help out in the kitchen, or do ironing.

One day, some weeks later, just before she began to read, her mistress handed her an envelope. She was dumbfounded – a letter from the mistress! It was indeed addressed to her, but she didn't recognise the handwriting, and she was even more confused as to why it was sent to her employer.

"Oh, Miss, I'm sorry the letter came to you; I can't imagine who could send me a letter." The sudden realisation that Rhoda was sick or even dead caused her knees to buckle; she cried out, "This isn't Ma's handwriting!"

"Sit down," said Arlene as she pushed her gently towards the nearest chair. "Don't panic; you won't know who sent it or what it's about unless you read it."

With trembling hands, she tore open the small white envelope, took out a large lined piece of paper, and began to read quietly, her lips moving silently with the words. Arlene sat on a chair facing her and watched as the girl's face transformed into deadly terror. She found herself shaking with the foreboding of bad news; she had never met Rhoda but had heard about her from Verna and felt she already knew her.

"Ma's sick; it's bad! My school teacher, Mrs Calder, wrote this; she said I must come home at once," she said through uncontrolled blubbering.

Arlene put an arm around her shoulders in a soft, supportive embrace, insisting she went home to her mother immediately. She rushed away to arrange for one of her family's smaller, faster yachts to take Verna home to her mother that very day.

As the top rim of the sun teased the horizon and the twilight lengthened the shadows on the restless, choppy sea, Verna arrived home filled with trepidation. She ran ahead of the small boy who was helping her with her bags, which were laden with food and medicines, all at Mrs Cassocks' behest. Molly Goodluck, Rhoda's closest friend and neighbour, was looking after her. Molly embraced Verna, then stood aside while the alarmed girl cradled her mother in her arms. After Molly left, having informed Verna that her mother was suffering from 'bad gut', she prepared some of the Milk of Magnesia she was given by Mrs Cassocks.

She looked on intently while her mother drank some of the thick, tasteless white liquid. Rhoda screwed up her face but began to feel a little better almost immediately. Perhaps it was her daughter's presence or the antacids and analgesics, but she was indeed beginning to recover. Verna never thought for a minute about Mrs Cassocks or her work while she was with her mother. At first, she felt relaxed as Rhoda recuperated, then began to worry about leaving her again.

"You got to go back soon, Verna; you got your job to do." Rhoda was sad, but reality had set in, they needed to eat.

"I know, Ma, but I wish I didn't have to go back and be so far away from you."

About a week later, a letter arrived from her boss. Seeing the name Arlene Cassocks signed at the bottom filled Verna with apprehension. She held the letter to her breast, too frightened to read it, but was encouraged by her mother to do so and see what was wanted of her; perhaps she was being ordered back to Bequia.

She walked down to the beach, its white sand glistening like millions of tiny diamonds under the glaring hot sun, her bare feet sinking so deep that it looked like she had no feet at all. She sat on a rotting hunk of an unfortunate coconut tree blown down years before by a strong tropical storm, incongruously lying on the pristine sand, and she began reading the enigmatic missive. She read it twice then ran up the incline back to the house where Rhoda, who had fully recovered but still a little gaunt, was frying red snapper fish for lunch. Verna joyously called out.

"Mrs Cassocks said to bring you with me to Bequia to see the doctor; she said he's very good. Then," she became animated, "she wants me to go to St Vincent with her, 'to accompany her,' she said."

There was quiet for a while from Rhoda, who didn't know how to react or what to say. Eventually, she found her voice and said incredulously, "Your rich mistress wants me to come to Bequia to see her doctor?"

"Yes, Ma, to get a checkup." The joy Verna felt about her mistress's generosity filled her with a giddy feeling.

"But we can't afford a doctor! I'm better now; I don't need a doctor. Tell your mistress that I'm better now and thank her for all the things she sent me." Rhoda was determined; she wasn't going to take up Mrs Cassocks' generous offer.

But Verna was fired up and insisted her mother take up the offer, which may never be repeated. Though she didn't say it aloud, she didn't want to miss the chance of travelling with the lovely, generous Mrs Cassocks to St Vincent.

As her mother pondered over leaving her home island even for a short time, Verna was eagerly anticipating the trip to St Vincent with her employer. She had no idea why she was needed there but was keen to find out. She eventually managed to coax Rhoda to accompany her back to Bequia.

Before Verna even got dressed and went to the kitchen to collect their breakfast, Arlene Cassocks knew via Bernice that they had returned. Verna was summoned to see her, and after breakfast she stood in front of her nervously awaiting instructions. Verna was told to take her mother to see the doctor at the public clinic that morning. She soon learnt the doctor had special clinics for the poor, but they may still have to pay for dispensed medicine.

According to Dr Edwards, a friend of the Cassocks who was thorough and kind, Rhoda was not as sick as they feared. He thought she had suffered a bacterial gut infection, and it got better naturally. He advised her to wash her hands properly after toilet use and to wash all the ground provisions, vegetables, meat and even fruits, before cooking and consuming. No picking a ripe plum, cherry, mango or guava straight from the tree and popping it into the mouth unwashed. Rhoda was baffled that something she did since childhood could be detrimental to her health now that she was older. She decided to ignore that doctoral order.

They listened politely and were taken aback when the good doctor shook their hands as they departed the clinic. They had never experienced this level of kindness from a white professional before.

"Nice man," said a grateful Rhoda, "I wish we had a permanent doctor back home, not one who comes and goes."

"Yes, that's why I want you here with me. It's better here than back home. If you get sick over there, you die before you get to see a doctor," said Verna.

She was worried for her mother; she feared that she would die horribly just like her grandmother did. She was little, but she remembered the groaning emanating from the restless old lady and Rhoda trying in vain to comfort her best she could. When her grandmother died, people said they were glad her suffering was over. She sometimes thought of her grandmother and winced, remembering the lead up to and that day she died in agony.

She had learnt a lot from books while reading to Mrs Cassocks and knew there were many diseases that could be deadly if they were not medically treated. She wanted Rhoda to be near help if she became ill again but feared her independent-minded mother would prefer nature to take its course rather than seek medical assistance. A day later, Rhoda returned to her home despite Verna's protestations.

Shortly afterwards, Verna and her mistress got ready to journey to St Vincent for a short visit. This was a dream come true, and though she had all but forgotten him, her mother asked her to pay her respects to Earl when or if she saw him.

At that moment she was not one bit interested in Earl but was dreaming of the adventures she would experience on the mainland. She forgot she was not a free spirit but a servant accompanying her mistress.

Chapter 2

Better Times

Verna's Adventure

The women settled down in the packed and larger than average schooner, which belonged to Arlene's husband's family and was one of the regular ferry boats that sailed between St Vincent and Bequia. As the hot sun bore down on their heads, the crowded boat, with its huge sails fluttering noisily in the brisk breeze, set sail for the main island. It was early morning when the schooner sailed out of Port Elizabeth's harbour and into open water between the two islands, Verna gasped as St Vincent loomed high and large in front of them. Arlene smiled at the young woman's childlike excitement.

An hour later, they arrived at Kingstown's red jetty, which lay in front of the large grey stoned, red roofed police station. As they disembarked, the jetty was already a hive of activity accompanied by deafening noises as people called to relatives and friends, stevedores unloaded and willing porters, shouted, fetched and carried. Rough wooden home-made carts with stout black rubber wheels, filled up with personal possessions and happily taken to the addresses indicated by grateful customers, for small monetary donations. Verna, laden with the goods they brought over, found herself walking briskly with her mistress towards the interior of the town.

She stared open-mouthed at the huge police station in front of them, the equally large court house, the Iron Man statue – commemorating the war dead from the past two world wars – proudly facing the main street, colloquially known as Back Street, the large stores and the noisy, crowded market. They soon arrived at their destination, and Arlene had to call Verna back because she had kept on walking, engrossed in the spectacle of the big, well-developed town. Almost immediately, she began dreaming of making this large town her future home.

Arlene's family was glad to see her; there was laughter and hugs, but Verna didn't see any of that. She was ushered through a high wooden but sturdy gate into the back of the large two-storey family home. Part of the first floor overhung the sidewalk beneath, thus forming an arch. These arches, which are unique to Kingstown, were a blessing to the local people as they rushed about their business, giving shelter from the hot sun and the all too frequent tropical showers. Verna was greeted by the equivalent of Bernice, only that this woman was younger and was called Hermie, who was surprised that the girl was so young – a child she thought.

Hermie was businesslike and showed Verna a small backroom, its door opening directly onto the backyard which would be her temporary abode. There was a narrow bed, a small dressing table without a mirror, a chair and very little spare space in the room. The other two doors outside were the entrances to a small shower and toilet for the staff's use. Hermie proceeded to instruct the bewildered young woman about what was expected of her and informed her that she was there to look after her mistress and to never enter any part of the house unless she was requested to do so.

Hermie was so authoritative in the way she spoke to her that she felt uneasy and wondered if the woman had taken an unwarranted dislike of her. Verna became afraid of the woman standing in front of her, though she reminded her of Elisha, but she mustered up the courage to ask her if she also lived there.

"No, I don't. Well, I am here during the daytime but sleep home in Paul's Lot wid my family. Don't worry, you are safe here at night. Just lock the door," she said in a friendlier tone.

Hermie's answer filled her with a quiet terror, there won't be any company during the night, she wished she was safely back in Bequia. It would be the first time in her life that she would be sleeping in a room quite alone. Hermie also explained more about the house routine and said she was flabbergasted as to why Mrs Cassocks brought her over; after all, there were only Mrs Cassocks' mother, Mrs Beryl Lorraine, and her sister, Miss Veronica Merriford, in residence. She added they also had another 'daily' woman coming in six days a week as well, and therefore, not a lot of extra work for anybody else to do in that large, four-bedroom home.

Verna wasn't listening; she was nervous about being alone during the night, and without realising it, she began to sniff. She wished Rhoda was there with her. Someone called out, and Hermie ran off towards the kitchen. Verna stood by the door of her temporary accommodation, feeling wretched.

Hermie poked her head around the kitchen's half-backdoor and called out, "Come, girl, come here!"

Verna walked quickly towards Hermie and entered a large kitchen filled with more paraphernalia than they had at the Bequia house. A woman about Hermie's age was standing by a side table unloading food shopping from a couple of large raffia baskets.

"Marlene, this is Verna; she came over from Bequia, too,"

she said with a little sarcasm.

Marlene turned and looked at the girl up and down as though she were a strange outer world creature. Then softened with a smile.

"Sit, girlie. Want a drink?" She pointed to a chair near the table, deducing Verna was a timid little thing. "Want some food?"

Hermie apologised, then rushed around to find something for the peckish girl to eat. As she ate, she began to feel more relaxed with the two older women and began to wonder why she was brought to this well-staffed household anyway. After the residents had had their lunch and the dining room and kitchen tidied and cleaned, the three maids sat outside in the backyard chatting under the shade of a large Bougainvillea tree. Verna was to learn, from these women, more about her mistress than she or any of the household staff back in Bequia knew about their employers.

Arlene Cassocks was born in that very house, the only child of Beryl and Dicky Lorraine, who once owned a couple of large stores in the town and cultivated lands in the country. Just after their daughter married a young man from a rich boat-owning family from Bequia, Mr Lorraine passed away suddenly. Her mother's only sibling, Veronica, had been living with the family for many years before Mr Lorraine died.

Arlene would come over to visit her mother and aunt several times a year; sometimes her husband Sidney accompanied her, and only Bernice, their cook, was privy to that knowledge. No one else in the household ever knew of their plans, but Verna did become aware of her sudden disappearance and reappearance again without explanation.

She couldn't understand why she was there at all but was

happy to get the opportunity to be on the main island nonetheless. Both her fellow workers promised her that they would take her around the town to get to know the place. To Verna, it was huge, and she couldn't wait to explore. She loved being in Kingstown and enjoyed working with the two older women. Whenever they had an errand to do or time off, they showed off the town and introduced her to more people than she could remember. She looked at the many outlets that could give her a job because, though she was grateful to her employers, she wanted more – a better job and a more rewarding life.

As she shadowed Hermie or Marlene around the town, she bravely asked them for advice about progressing to another level and got some stark reminders of the realities of life.

"You got qualifications?" Hermie had asked.

No, she didn't have any but felt that a willingness to learn and work hard would be an advantage. Unfortunately, Hermie was unable to see how a girl in her position without qualifications, family or friends with connections could get beyond her present station.

Verna was surprised at how little she saw her mistress or how little her contribution to the housework was; she was puzzled, but on the whole, she enjoyed being in Kingstown. Then, a few days before they were due to return to Bequia, she remembered Earl, but neither Hermie nor Marlene knew or heard of him. Marlene was dead sure no man called Earl was living in Kingstown, perhaps not even in St Vincent. But she did concede that there were many young men wandering around the town most days of the week looking for work, and the only person she heard called Earl was a little bitty boy up the road.

"What he looks like?" asked Hermie.

"Oh, not sure. I was ten when he left Mayron; he just looked like any teenage boy, I guess." She was racking her memory bank, trying to remember what Earl looked like then.

"Well, he'd be a grown man now, so he'd look different; he could be walking right in front of you and you don't know," said Marlene.

"But surely he'd remember me!" Verna asserted.

"No, he won't; just tink, you don't look ten any more; you are a woman now; dat is a big difference."

Verna had to agree with her colleagues that Earl would look as different to her as she would be to him. She was sorry that she wouldn't be able to meet up with him and wished she had some good news to share with her mother. She hoped he was abroad somewhere and not dead; she couldn't believe Marlene knew everyone in Kingstown and therefore hoped Earl was somewhere safe out there.

On their penultimate day, Arlene attended church with her family, followed by lunch with her mother's family members on Dorsetshire Hill, a place of scattered houses on a hill overlooking east Kingstown. Verna was in the house alone; the other maids either took that day off or went away while the family was not at home. Being left alone, she decided to have a leisurely walk around the town. She wanted to breathe in the atmosphere one more time, though it being Sunday, the commercial heart of the capital was quite dead.

She went down to the bay front, then walked the length of bay street towards the eastern end of Kingstown. She turned back, briefly pausing to look at the lovely things decoratively displayed in store windows, then turned north and entered the deserted Middle street. She continued her leisurely stroll back to the house on this deserted street when a vaguely familiar voice called her name, startling her.

"Verna, is that you?" The male voice knew her name.

She quickened her steps away from the man who was approaching her. But even though there was a slight familiarity about the figure, she accelerated her pace anyway.

"It's me, Earl," he called out, "don't you remember me? You were quite small when I left Mayron years ago." She softened in recognition of the voice.

Earl? She stopped and looked closely at the softly spoken man in front of her, realising in that instant that it was indeed Earl from back home. He was taller than her, a little too skinny but well-groomed in well-pressed brown trousers and a dazzlingly white buttoned-down short-sleeved shirt and gold-looking rings adorning some of his fingers. Verna's mouth opened slowly in awe.

"Yes, it's me; I can't believe it, little Verna, all grown up! You live here; how come I never bumped into you before?" he spoke in a rush, his heart pounding. He was amazed at the beauty standing in front of him.

"No I don't live here just visiting, I live in Bequia, going back tomorrow." She burst into tears as confusion welled up inside.

Earl consoled her and tenderly dried her eyes with a clean white handkerchief he pulled out of his pocket. As they walked slowly back to her destination, she filled him in on her life in the near decade they were apart. When they got to the house, they stood by the gate talking, and both expressed regrets they would be parted again so soon. Verna started to cry again.

"Don't cry; we'll meet again soon." His voice trembled with emotion.

"When would that be then? Oh, Earl, I'm missing here already!"

"I shouldn't have ignored my friends! Tell Anty Rhoda I miss her."

A car pulled up, the family had returned, Verna bade Earl farewell with a quick peck on his hollow cheek, then rushed through the gate. She was heartbroken; she couldn't stop crying. If only she had met him before, she probably would have abandoned Mrs Cassocks and stayed permanently in St Vincent; she was filled with regret.

The next day, Arlene and Verna stood on the crowded jetty waiting to board the schooner that would take them back to Bequia. The early morning sun was peering over Dorsetshire Hill, bathing Kingstown in an increasingly hot glow. The town was rising, and both women were silently praying for a quick, safe journey; the sea was a little too choppy.

Earl pushed his way through the crowded jetty, found the ladies, and thrush a small packet into Verna's hand.

"For you and anty. Good voyage." He brushed a kiss on Verna's cheek, then disappeared.

A tingle rushed down her spine like nothing she had experienced before; tears clouded her vision; she felt utterly bereft. She tried to pull herself together in front of her mistress, confused as to why a man she had not seen since childhood could stir such intense feelings.

The women were sitting astern in the boat, which sat low in the water with people and goods. It slowly pushed outwards then began gathering speed in the brisk wind, on occasion bearing precariously low on its starboard side; its sails seemed dangerously close to touching the saltwater as it manoeuvred through the mid-channel's rolling rough waves. Verna was relieved when the boat straightened as it sailed around Bequia's headland into calmer waters.

She couldn't stop the tears dropping onto her lap, not because of the rough sea journey but at losing Earl again. Their brief encounter had her confused; she began to speculate whether there would be another island, another life in her future, and whether Earl would be a part of it. Arlene had seen the encounter with the young man and wondered what his connection was to Verna. She felt strangely discomfited; she had a niggling feeling; things were going to change for all of them.

There was so much to tell Elisha, Bernice and anyone else who would listen. Verna bored them all with her Kingstown adventure, and more than ever she was determined to leave quiet Bequia for Kingstown's dazzling lights. She wrote her mother a long letter accompanied with the pure cotton hankies Earl sent for her, the letter gushed about the suave young man who literally swept her off her feet. Elisha got tired of hearing about handsome, suave Earl and reminded Verna that the man she met may be a jailbird. But if Verna was really honest, she would have said he was scrawny with a hollow gaunt face.

"He said he owns a barbershop and he looks the part. He got money in his pocket." Verna crossed her fingers because he was groomed and smartly dressed, she was sure he must be doing well he looked like someone with prospects.

"What about a wife? A man his age is bound to have a wife or girlfriend or something." Elisha seemed determined to put Verna off a possible future with Earl.

"If he had someone in his life, he would have said. I feel it in my bones; he's the one for me. A boy from back home, done well." She was beaming with joy and placed a hand tenderly over her heart.

Elisha gave up. She felt an overpowering sense of emotions as Verna walked away but hoped life showed the ambitious young lady a better hand than it did for her.

Before Verna began to read at their next session, Arlene mischievously asked, "So, what do you think of Kingstown?"

"Oh, lovely, Miss! So many stores, the huge courthouse, the police station, the big churches – so many things to see and do. I wish I lived there. This place is dead in comparison." Then, remembering where she was and who she was talking to, she apologised for being so rudely outspoken.

Arlene burst out laughing, sending Verna into a whirl of confusion. She flopped back into the chair with a resigned air at the realisation that she was being laughed at. However, there was renewed delight in her reading, and Arlene wondered if it had anything to do with the young man on the jetty. She had been so preoccupied with her mother and her woes that she didn't pay much attention to Verna, and now she felt the girl had had more fun than she did, and she couldn't help feeling a little jealous.

Some weeks later, as she ate her lunch sitting under the lime tree with Elisha, she decided to leave her employment and move to the main island permanently. Earl was her future and not this poor slavish work she was forced to undertake through no fault of hers. She was sure that if she had been raised on the main island, she would have had a better education and a more promising future. Elisha was appalled by Verna's willpower, but deep down she hoped things worked out for this lovely determined teenager.

"You what!" Arlene was taken aback when Verna gave notice to leave her employment.

"Yes, Miss, I'm going back; I like it there; I feel at home over there." Then she dropped her head in contrition, as though she had done something awful.

Arlene felt cornered but didn't want to appear churlish, so

gave her permission to leave any time and wished her well. This willingness to let her go had Verna in a spin; she had expected a barracking but got pleasantness instead. Back in her room, she wrote two letters, one to her mother and the other to Earl.

"Ah know yuh hankering over dat man; hope to God he is not married or someting. Yuh don't know nothin 'bout him, but ah wish yuh well anyway." Elisha was pragmatic, but she thought Verna's decision was fraught with uncertainty and maybe danger; she worried about her hot-headedness.

When Rhoda received the letter, it was filled with gushing news of the new life her daughter planned on the main island with or without Earl. Rhoda was horrified, her heart bursting with fear for her daughter's rashness. Earl was a good boy growing up on Mayron, but what sort of man did he become over there, she wondered.

Rhoda replied, begging Verna to be cautious and to stop thinking of Earl as the answer to all her prayers; a brief acquaintance was no basis for long-term planning. She reminded her of her youth and implored her to come home if she was tired of servant work. But Verna was adamant; she had made up her mind, had her future firmly mapped out, and no one, not even her mother, was going to scupper her intentions.

Aspirations

It was not until she arrived in Kingstown a few days later that the realisation hit her that if Earl didn't get her letter, she would be stranded. She had sent the letter via the post office and hoped he would get it anyway. She stood waiting on the emptying jetty for him. Once everyone had gone, she picked up her grip and the two baskets she brought with her and began walking upright and dignified towards Middle street. She soon arrived at the very spot she met him that Sunday, a few months before.

She became aware of a few curious glances, then braced herself to ask a lady selling combs, hair grips, and bits and pieces for personal ladies care laid out on the ground if she knew Earl, but the lady never even heard of him. She walked up and down the town, asking anyone she met if they knew him. It became a long, fruitless task. Later that afternoon, totally exhausted and feeling humiliated, she went to Mrs Cassocks' mother's home and rang the doorbell. Hermie's lower jaw dropped when she saw Verna. She looked behind her, thinking Mrs Cassocks had come unannounced to visit her mother.

"No, it's just me. I come over alone," Verna said, then added, "for good!" She couldn't hold it in any more; she began to weep with exhaustion and disappointment. Hermie took her around the back of the house and into the kitchen. She poured a cold glass of freshly made lemonade juice from the fridge, handed it over to the shaken young woman, and then waited for her to recover. And what a story she had to tell! Hermie was amazed by the girl's stupidity but admired her determination. She wanted to help but didn't know what to say or do but said she knew of someone who may be able to help and that she'd call on her after her work shift ended.

Verna couldn't possibly stay at the house, so Hermie took her home to meet her family and to squash in with them. The poverty she saw at Hermie's was reminiscent of her childhood; she felt lonely and bewildered. She mused, Elisha and her mother were right; she was too reckless, fantasising about a life that would be impossible for a girl like her to attain.

Next morning Hermie left for work just after dawn. Verna

was left with Leila, Hermie's daughter, who was about her age and already had a baby son. The unemployed Leila was friendly and took Verna under her wing; later that morning she walked with her through the streets of Kingstown, hoping to find the elusive Earl.

Hermie, Leila, her son Troy, Hermie's son Byron and Verna sat in their tiny yard on the near-rotting rickety wooden steps of their ramshackle home, eating rice and peas with the bony fish Leila had acquired from the fish market earlier. Verna was grateful for their hospitality and knew she had to start job hunting the very next day or starve; she couldn't possibly impose herself on these nice, struggling people for too long.

"I asked my friend Hessie, and she say if you have no qualifications these days, it's hard to get 'good' work. You try stores and things or go back to domestic work."

Hermie looked at the two young women in front of her, one cradling her baby, abandoned by its father, facing a bleak future of no more than subsistence living and the other craving for a chance to improve herself and reach a higher platform of life.

"Verna," she said helpfully, "try asking at all the stores, small shops, offices, anything, you might get lucky. And try the hospital—"

"But I don't want to nurse; I feel bad around sick—" she interrupted.

"Listen, young lady," Hermie was beginning to get impatient with the little too fussy Verna, "you hear the saying 'beggars can't be choosers' well, you try everything and do anything when you're starving. You can't expect a top job widout qualifications. You look good and talk well, but you need a piece of paper to say that your education is good too."

Verna bowed her head in shame and promised she would try

everywhere possible until she found something. How, she thought, could she face Rhoda if she pushed them further into impoverishment? Leila cradled her baby and kept her eyes fixed on the ground. She had not bothered with school much and defied her mother when she begged her to get a better education than she did. She listened to her mother admonishing Verna and felt embarrassed, feeling that it was a veiled criticism directed at her. All they had to alleviate the poverty-stricken position they wallowed in was her mother's meagre domestic wage.

At the end of another fruitless day and after she had walked her well-worn sandals even thinner and her feet hurt with blisters, she was sadder than she had ever been. As usual, they all sat in the same place, eating their supper from battered enamel dishes. The 'Bolleen' soup which Leila made was filled with ground provisions; the yam was a little tough and the eddoes slippery in their mouths, but it was delicious.

Verna moaned that no business seemed to want to give her a job, not even the dark, cramped Middle street shops to the west of the town. She reluctantly decided that she'd abandon her aspirations for office or shop work and return to domestic service. She would try looking in all of Kingstown's suburbs: Murray Village, Kingstown Park, Frenches, Sion Hill, Cane Garden, New Montrose and even Edinboro settlement, which lay under the old fortified Fort Charlotte, which looked over Kingstown from its high hilltop.

Hermie felt sad for her and hoped she would be successful in attaining an office or shop work. This young girl, she reflected, should do something better than servant work. Poor Hermie was feeling a little desperate, wanting Verna to find work quickly, not wanting her to experience Leila's fate.

"Tomorrow," she said, "you must go to Rose Place. Marlene

say a man called Mr Wellman got a big shop down there and wants somebody to help him because his wife was too sick to work. If he says no, then go to the hospital and see if they have work for cleaners, kitchen staff and suchlike. Leila, show Verna way to go."

"Yes, Mother, ah show her," replied a chastened Leila wishing she too could find work but not until she found someone trustworthy to look after her baby.

The very next day, the two young women ambled from Paul's Lot towards Bottom Town, where the hospital was also located in the far west of Kingstown and just below Edinboro Hill. Leila carried her son in her arms and seemed to know everyone they met, stopping a little too often, for Verna's liking, for a chat. They crossed the bridge and were almost there and quite close to Mr Wellman's shop when Verna saw a notice stuck to the closed gate outside a large, official-looking building.

"Hey, wait a minute, Leila, what's this?" She read the notice a few times, then told Leila she was going inside to ask for a job. The notice just said there were vacancies within but not what they were. She pushed and walked through the huge black wooden gates towards the back of the building but was accosted by a security guard who asked her sternly why she was there. Taken aback by the greying man's aggression, she timidly said she was going to ask about the vacancies advertised on the gate. He relented, opened the door they were standing near, and ushered her in.

Leila waited patiently outside the building for a short while before wandering off with little restless Troy. However, it wasn't long before Verna exited the building; she looked around anxiously and unsuccessfully for Leila, then returned to Paul's Lot. She threw her grip open and took out the one decent dress inside, her 'Sunday' dress. She took out her one good pair of shoes too because she wanted to look good for her interview. It was over an hour when Leila returned home.

"So, you back then," she said to Leila when she entered the little yard in front of the house with Troy. "I couldn't find you when I left the building."

"Yeh, been to see my friend Aggie, just down the road from that building you went into and forgot how she could talk. Anyway, you get a job?" Leila saw the dress hanging just inside the window frame and the 'good' shoes laid out beneath it.

"That was a government building, the department for public works that I went into. The notice said they wanted staff, and the nice lady I saw said to come back tomorrow for an interview."

"What, you got a job?" Leila was incredulous.

"No, not yet; I'm having an interview," Verna stressed. "I'll take any job they offer me, cleaning, kitchen work, anything!"

An Office Job

Leila was happy for Verna but couldn't help thinking that she wouldn't see much of her if she got regular work; she liked being in her company. Verna was lucky; a tiny prim lady, Mrs Walcott, was the interviewer. Despite her demeanour, this lady was progressive; she wanted to give ambitious young people a chance and could see in Verna a clever, articulate addition to the department's workforce. She was interviewed long and in depth, and Mrs Walcott was not fazed by the young lady's lack of school certificates, and by the time it was over, she had a job as an office junior: running errands and being the general dogsbody.

She was so overjoyed that she got a job in an office that

anyone would have been forgiven for thinking she just landed the manager's job. She hurried back to Paul's Lot and found Leila busily making mushy food for Troy.

"I got it! I got a job in a government office." She danced, dripping with sweat after running back to Paul's Lot in the hot sun.

"Oh, Lard, you're going to work in a big government place. Now you a big shot, you won't want to know me!" Leila feared losing the one true friend she ever had, even though they only knew each other a few weeks.

Hermie hugged and kissed the thrilled young lady; she was glad to have her with them and didn't mind her squashing in but knew it wouldn't be forever. She couldn't see her wanting to live with them once she moved up in the world.

It didn't take long for Verna to get the hang of her unskilled work, which she took to with enthusiasm. Everyone at the office liked her politeness and her willingness to learn. Every day as she walked out of Paul's Lot in the town centre, she sang silently with joy about her good fortune. She couldn't wait to tell her mother about her good luck acquiring her dream job in an office. Mrs Walcott felt she was exceptionally clever and therefore wasted. She also loved the girl's honesty; she didn't hold back anything about her life when she was asked during the interview. She decided to give Verna a helping hand towards promotion when two positions would eminently be vacant.

Verna was nearly four months into her new job when she was called into Mrs Walcott's office for a 'quick chat,' she had said. Unsure whether it was for a rollicking or praise, she went in and respectfully stood in front of her supervisor and waited. To her surprise, she was congratulated on her work, and her boss stunned her with her next words.

"You're a good worker, Verna, and we all like your diligence. However, if you want promotion, you'll have to learn to type."

This was a higher mountain than she had ever envisaged; she had been happy with what she had been assigned to do and thought that was as far as she would get without proper qualifications. She had an office job, her dream all along, and more was being handed to her on a plate. She wasn't sure she could handle that sort of elevation.

"I don't think I'm good enough for typing." She blinked nervously.

"Nonsense! I'll send you to a friend of mine who'll teach you how to type. She's affordable; you'd be fine. Stop worrying, young lady."

A couple of weeks later, on a very hot Saturday morning, and with the address, instructions and the day's tuition fee in her little pocketbook, she walked slowly to her destination up Mackies Hill. This hill and the scattered houses dotted precariously on it overlooked the town from a north-easterly aspect, with Paul's Lot directly beneath. By the time she reached the house, almost on top of the steep hill, she was sweating, breathless and trembling with fear.

Miss Honey, who had retired from the civil service and made a modest living by teaching young females etiquette, cooking, baking, sewing, crocheting and typing on most Saturdays throughout the year, was an old friend of Mrs Walcott. Through Mrs Walcott, she had already known all about Verna and her low financial situation, but nevertheless, she welcomed her with friendly candour.

There were a few young women busy beavering away at various tasks when she entered the mini school that Saturday morning. She was taken to a table, shared by a few other girls, to sit in front of a large, high black instrument. It was daunting to her because though she had seen these instruments at work, she had never touched one, except to wipe the dust off one of her jobs at the office. The patient, Miss Honey, in a gentle, encouraging voice, began her tuition by showing Verna how to sit upright and focus in front of the formidable machine. She was quite flabbergasted with the amount she had to learn and was sure she would never master such a complicated apparatus.

When she got home later, she was filled with misgivings. She described in graphic detail her ordeal during that first lesson at Miss Honey's to Hermie and Leila. She swore never to go back because it was way above her capabilities. The wise Hermie encouraged her to keep going because with practice and as time passed, it would get easier. Though Verna reluctantly agreed to continue her studies, she wondered if she had the intellect after all. Every day while she cleaned the Cassocks home, she had craved formal learning to better herself, but as the new dawn of betterment presented itself, she became frightened of achieving that goal after all and wanted to flee from the angst.

At work, she found the rapid tap-taping of the working typewriters around her intimidating. Each tap reminded her of her inability to grasp the correlation of eyes, to lettered keys, to rolling paper, which the ladies in her office seem to handle with effortless skill. Whenever Mrs Walcott asked her how the lessons were coming along, she fibbed and said she couldn't wait to become a fully fledged typist.

She eventually moved on from Hermie and her family when she became a lodger at Mrs Darrow's Old Montrose home. This lady rented rooms to out-of-town young women who needed a place to stay while they worked in the capital. After her husband's sudden death, she needed to supplement her paltry income; her spare rooms were continuously occupied thereafter. Verna knew that sooner or later she had to leave Hermie's, and though it was a tight squeeze there, she didn't want to upset her benevolent friends. Hermie didn't ask for rent or hinted it was a tight squeeze in her tiny home, but Verna pressed a little money in her grateful hands each payday regardless.

A work colleague who once boarded at Mrs Darrow's had moved into her own place and quietly told Verna that the widow had a vacancy. She pointed out to Verna that it was far preferable to living in Paul's Lot, which in parts had a bad reputation and unsavoury types causing trouble in that poor corner of the capital. She was told that the house was a newish brick building and that the sanitary arrangements were inside the building and private and therefore better than sharing the public facilities in questionable state in the rundown area she currently lived in.

When she arrived in Kingstown alone and friendless, she was rescued and looked after by Hermie and her family and was comfortable in their company. However, she was soon tired – though she didn't show it – of the poverty of the situation and wanted better. She was grateful for Hermie's charity but found it difficult to tell her that it was time she moved on to better things. Leila was full of sadness as she watched Verna pack her few meagre things in her small grip, ready to move to Old Montrose, a suburb north of Kingstown with a deep but narrow river flowing through it. The area had a mixture of residents of various economic levels, and the Darrow's home stood out in its newness and substantial pride from its poorer neighbours.

Verna slept like a log on her first night in Old Montrose. The gentle rumble of the river with its busy water rushing over the big boulders scattered haphazardly on its slippery bed did not disturb her relaxed mood. She didn't miss having Elisha to chat with while they lay in their shared darkened room in Bequia or Leila and her baby fidgeting beside her on the floor in Paul's Lot, but she did miss her mother terribly.

In her new room with its white smooth-walled cleanness, there was a single-door wardrobe, a four-drawer dressing table with a round mirror which smoothly swung in whatever position it was needed in, and a narrow bedside table to accompany her comfortable single bed. The rent was just a little more than she used to give to Hermie, and she could still save something for her typing lessons. She was usually penniless before the end of each month but still coped quite well because she didn't socialise but spent a great deal of her spare time at Mrs Darrow's indulging in her favourite pastime, reading. The town library became her favourite place of recreation. Verna read every genre of book; she just loved books.

Mrs Darrow was a staunchly Christian woman who didn't gossip and treated her boarders like hotel guests. She and a daily helper cooked and cleaned and made sure her boarders were comfortable and happy. She never asked probing questions about themselves or their families but insisted on knowing where they worked and in what capacity.

However, she was concerned about their ability to pay the rent and made sure it was presented to her on the appointed day. The boarders liked her non-intrusiveness and were respectful to her. She did, however, point out to them that no males were allowed in the house; anyone breaking this rule was evicted immediately. Needless to say, Verna got the full rules and regulations spiel, which she promised to keep when she first met Mrs Darrow.

She lived further away from her job, typing lessons, the town centre and Paul's Lot, but blazing tropical heat, rain or howling wind never halted her ladylike walk out of Old Montrose. Walking in a straight-backed dignified manner, she took the long, straight road out of Old Montrose that took her past the Botanic Gardens, New Montrose, the convent and its school, the cheerless Gothically imposing Roman Catholic Church on the riverside of the road, and the cheerier Gothic Anglican Cathedral on the other side. Both churches face each other in friendly rivalry.

At the end where River Road met Grenville Street, popularly called Back Street, Verna would turn left eastwards towards the town centre, pass Paul's Lot and the court house on one side and the market on the other, then up the steep hill to Miss Honey's. She at last began to look forward to her weekly lessons because she was improving; she was beginning to understand the daunting instrument in front of her.

The day Miss Honey said a joyful 'well done' was the day Verna knew she had made it. She was told her forty words a minute were adequate, but she must strive for up to seventy to be able to achieve a secretarial post. She had not thought that was possible for a long time and had put promotion out of her mind. She was starting to accept that the level she was at work was not too bad for an ex-maid.

She sat at Mrs Darrow's dining table with the fountain pen she was given at work poised in her hand, a laid-out sheet of paper on an exercise book, and began to write to her mother. She had not written to Rhoda for months except when she first got the office job. She had not abandoned her mother, but she felt she didn't have much to say before, but as she began to write, she was more confident and hopeful of the path her life was moving in.

The most important story to divulge was about her great

improvement at typing, the probability of promotion to the typing pool, and earning a bit more money. She wrote at length about her living conditions, the friends she was making, and her sorrow for Leila and Hermie, whose lives were forever blighted by the stark ongoing poverty enveloping them. When she wrote about Hermie's family, she acknowledged her own mother's poverty. She put a few dollars in the envelope with the letter but knew it wasn't enough to lift Rhoda much higher than she was presently enduring.

Come over, Mama, Mrs Darrow said she can put you up. There are lots of opportunities over here, and I need you here with me, she had written. She daydreamed that she and her mother could find a nice house like the one she was living in, and with the prospect of promotion, they should be able to afford an upgrade.

Life was improving faster for Verna than she had ever thought possible. She reached the required typing standard, and luckily for her, a vacancy arose immediately when an older woman at the office retired. There was a string of upward promotions, and she was admitted to the typing pool – well, just three other ladies on a shared desk forever typing out reams of government papers. She was conscious of her slower typing skills but admired the swiftness of her colleagues' fingers on the typewriters' keys, praying she would soon be as adept as they were.

Rhoda was impressed with her daughter's progression and of all the positive things she wrote about what had happened to her, so she decided to visit her to see for herself. However, before making a decision whether to leave Mayron or not, she went to the cemetery and 'discussed' her future with her dead relatives. Afterwards, she made the momentous decision to move to

Kingstown permanently to be at her child's side.

Before leaving Mayron, she packed up all her belongings in several small crates: the few decent glasses, crockery, cutlery, bed linen and her meagre personal items, such as photographs and clothes, ready for shipment to the main island. She went to Mrs Lamour, her landlady and boss, to let her know she was leaving their cosy little island, then bade farewell to all her friends, especially Molly Goodluck, which really broke her heart.

Verna's resourceful forty-year-old mother soon settled into Kingstown's life with startling ease. She rapidly acquired a job at the general hospital as a nursing aide. Several months later, she and Verna left Mrs Darrow and moved into a small, furnished, two-bedded riverside residence further along river road that they could just manage to rent between them. This recently refurbished wooden house, which was covered in painted grey wooden slats, had a bright red galvanised roof, two wooden front windows, and a tiny porch with two steps almost touching the asphalted road at the front. There were two doors at the riverside back, one to an indoor shower and flush toilet and the other, split in two halves, to the attached kitchen. In the cramped, narrow backyard, there was room for a clothesline and an outdoor sink and water tap, but the small, stony area was mostly full of weeds.

Both ladies thought they had hit the jackpot and had just moved into a palace, which they rented from Mrs Williams of Lower Middle Street, an acquaintance of Mrs Darrow. This was a wonderful little house, perfectly befitting a mother who never had such a good home before and a daughter whose sights were aimed even higher. The rumbling river beneath their Jalousie windows didn't hamper the joy they felt that first night they settled to sleep peacefully on their separate beds in their own rooms in their own home on river road.

Chapter 3

Slim – Earl's Forward Step

Searching

Sitting on his narrow veranda that overlooked the street beneath, Earl fiddled with the numerous rings on his fingers while surveying the horizon before him. He was content with his lot – a wife, two children, a successful business and his own home. He had long forgotten the tiny island in the Grenadines he once called home and the naïve Verna he accidentally met in Kingstown well over two years before. As far as he was concerned, Mayron was past life; he had moved on; his move to the main island had been the making of him, but not at first.

When he arrived in Kingstown years ago in 1950, a hungry, penniless teenager, he was full of anger for the years of suffering he and his mother Rosanna had endured. It wasn't easy; he begged for work and shelter, and it was quite a while before he was able to find interim work. He cleaned the dirty market floor after it emptied six days a week, and sometimes he weeded, pruned the gardens, and cleaned the yards of residents who took pity on him for measly cash or a plate of food. At night he sheltered under a one-room hut, which was the abode of a lady called Pearl, who took pity on him and even fed him when he didn't find work or had money to buy food. That was his precarious way of living until he had a lucky break.

In Rose Place, also known as Bottom Town, in a rundown area called 'The Alley', he felt at home amid the poor and disadvantaged people who lived there. Middle Street, which like Back Street and Bay Street, ran the entire length of Kingstown, divided the two halves of Bottom Town and ended where the high steps known as Nine Steps ended. These high, wide concrete steps, some said sixty, others said the ascent felt like a hundred, ascended from the very end of Middle Street and ended at the top on Edinboro Road, which snaked around the hill to the Edinboro settlements.

A few hundred yards along, this road splits into two branches, one descending to the small seaside settlement of Lower Edinboro and the other continuing on to Upper Edinboro with a few scattered dwellings bordering both sides of the road. Eventually, the road ended at the old fortifications of Fort Charlotte, complete with old cannons, which once, in bygone days, were used to protect the English-owned island from the marauding French.

Some Saturdays, after hours of trying to find something worthwhile to do and failing, he would return back to Bottom Town tired, hungry and dejected. He would hang around the steps, observing the comings and goings, and listen to the 'loud mouths', as Pearl observed her neighbours, causing a raucous. Without fail, people gathered, talking, laughing and enjoying the company, but there were times when high-spirited behaviour ended in fisticuffs, screaming and sometimes a full-scale riot.

On some of those carefree or hectic days, a big, amiable man everyone called Leroy arrived with his stool and a wooden box containing his instruments to cut men's and boys' hair for a minimal charge. With nothing better to do, Earl would observe the barber cutting hair. He noticed the happiness around as the big guy talked and speedily clipped his customers' tight curls. Earl ran his hand over his massive cloud of knotted hair and craved a haircut, which he couldn't afford. One day he took a deep breath and asked the big man if he could have a haircut.

"Fifty cents, you got a big head of hair, man," said Leroy.

"All ah got is tutty cents, sah." He lowered his head in embarrassment.

"When you get fifty, come back." Leroy wasn't budging.

"All right, sah, ah come back." He turned solemnly away and walked towards Pearl's rickety, tiny hut.

In St Vincent, many people, mostly men, had nicknames. These were usually given to suit the person's personality or demeanour, and due to his thin, half-starved frame, Earl's nickname became Slim, which he accepted without rancour. With the exception of his friend Pearl, no one knew his real name was Earl Drake. He sat down on the bare, hardened earth next to Pearl's coal pot. She gave him a damaged enamel plate of rice covered in greasy gravy with a few bits of saltfish, which she was happy to share with him.

He was grateful and also helpful to her, fetching water from the standpipe on the corner or sweeping up the dusty area around her home. He realised, as he spooned the food from the battered plate, that he could never afford a barber and decided the only thing to do was cut his own hair, which had grown into a great mass of tangles. However, he had to acquire a pair of scissors first. The next day he was up from under the hut at dawn, washed his face with the little drop of water in the bucket near Pearl's front door, refilled the bucket at the standpipe, then hurried off to the market in the town centre.

The market was already getting busy, and Earl hoped he would be lucky to get some work. His dream was to earn steady money, live indoors and sleep on a proper bed. He was lucky that day; the market manager had him running around doing the odd jobs that were available that day. He had been in the capital a couple of years and had nothing to show for it, just rags for clothes, a worn pair of sandals from which he could feel the ground on his naked feet, and no regular place to live. He often wished he could send a Christmas card to Rhoda and Verna but couldn't afford to, and, as time passed, he forgot Mayron and the friends he left there.

Working diligently, he had twenty dollars in his one secure pocket by the end of that day and joy in his heart. He was exhausted and hungry and plonked himself heavily on the ground near Pearl, who was sitting on a low stool in front of her coal pot. They smiled at each other, and Pearl handed him a plate of food she had just prepared.

"Here, son, you look all done in."

"Oh, this looks good," he said, licking his lips.

He had only eaten the odd discarded piece of fruit and a peanut-coated sugar-cake or two that day, and his stomach cried out for something more substantial. Pearl had roasted a breadfruit and had fried some fresh sprats, which she got for free from a fisherman who knew her quite well, when the nets were pulled in on Bottom Town's dark sand beach. He knew she couldn't afford the healthy-looking fish in the nets, jacks, red snapper and an assortment of other sea creatures, including sea crabs. The two of them ate with relish; it was a feast. Pearl was sickly and couldn't work, but she received a little government subsistence, which didn't go far enough; if it wasn't for her richer good neighbours who lived on Back Street, her gut would grumble with hunger.

Afterwards, Earl took the empty tin dishes and washed them from the bucket, then he sat down again, drinking a large enamel cup of sweetened cocoa tea. Though he was grateful to Pearl for giving him shelter, he craved some comfort. He had had enough of sleeping under her house with only a layer of cardboard between him and the bare earth. He shared the space with ants, numerous other creepy crawlies, busy small green lizards, noisy crickets, buzzing mosquitoes and the odd stray dog for company.

"Miss Pearl, ah got a couple of dollars for you." He handed her a well-used, crumpled-up dollar bill.

"No, Slim, you need it more." She was thinking of his huge head of hair that needed cutting, his ragged clothes and his semi-bare feet caked in dirt.

"You good to me, Miss Pearl; feed me when ah hungry, a friend when ah got none. Make me happy, take it, please!"

She took the money, shedding a tear not only for Earl but for her good fortune having such a caring young man at her side. They sat chatting until the dusk began to darken everything, then she retreated into her hut. Though he was tired, he decided to go for a stroll on the seafront before bedding down for the night with the insect and animal world. He saw a small crowd of men and women standing outside a popular rum shop, talking, laughing and obviously tipsy from imbibing cheap rum. He tentatively walked past the group but was called back by a voice he recognised.

"Hey Slim, come here. I want to ask you something." It was Leroy the barber.

The big charismatic, popular small-time businessman towered over Earl and draped his arms around his bony shoulders. They walked off from the others, and Leroy talked of how he admired the young man's tenacity in searching out a better living for himself and hoped it would pay off. He told Earl about the time when he first came to Kingstown from an inland village called Mesopotamia and how desperately he searched for work. He begged and starved, and one day he came across an old man cutting hair in a tiny shop in Sion Hill. He stood outside and, through a small window, watched and begged to be taught until the man, taking pity, took him on to clean up the shop, then eventually to become his pupil. Earl wasn't sure where the narrative was taking him, so he stopped walking and said he needed to get home.

"Home!" Leroy's voice boomed out in the darkness. "You homeless Slim, you got nothing!"

Earl was not the kind of person who roused to anger easily but he thought Leroy was laughing at him. He shook himself free from the big man's grasp and with a quiet dignity upbraided him.

"Don't mock me; ah know ah got no job, no nice clothes and no room to lay down at night, but ah have dignity." He shook with anger.

"Hey Slim, just saying I know how you feel cause I was in that same boat once. Now I gat a business, a wife, children and a nice house."

"But you only cut poor people's hair; yuh can't make much!" Earl became more puzzled than angry.

"I have a nice barbershop in Arnos Vale. You know where that is?"

"Ah hear it ova by Sion Hill," he replied, trying to sound knowledgeable.

"Nay, way past Sion Hill, then down the valley to Arnos Vale," corrected Leroy. He explained how he went to places in and around town on Saturdays to cut hair for what little money poor people could afford and that sometimes he did it for free.

"Boy, I am giving you a job to help me cut hair!" Then looking over Earl's massive head of hair, he said with a wide, toothy grin. "Ah do you first, for free!"

Earl stood dumbfounded in front of the big man, unable to react. He had waited for a long time for a job, but as one was thrust on him, he didn't know how to respond. He had never imagined being a barber but saw himself more as a store worker, someone organising the market, or even a dock worker at the harbour, all of which he tried to get employment for without success.

"Well, what do you think?" The big man boomed again.

"Thanks, Mr Leroy. When ah start?" he asked, visibly shaking with anticipation.

"Meet me down by Nine Steps Saturday afternoon, right where you ask me to cut your hair."

Though he was tired, Earl lay on his back under Pearl's house, waiting for sleep. His head whirling with thoughts of his future, sometime in the dark, stifling night he drifted off into a deep sleep. It was the cacophony of sounds – people's voices, the big boobie bird calls, people shouting, dogs barking and the fusion of confusing smells – that roused him.

He rushed to the bucket to wash the sleep out of his eyes, rushed to the busy communal toilet, and was about to rush off when Pearl stopped him. She handed him the large enamel cup of cocoa tea she had prepared and a small, dry, crusty loaf. He drank the hot tea in record time and walked off with the loaf in his hand. He was late for work at the market; he had to dash. Pearl watched his departing, wiry body run down the road and hoped he would be lucky. Like most low-paid temporary work, it always depended on who arrived first when the market or other outlets were opening up.

He wasn't lucky. All the other unemployed, uneducated and, as Earl called them and himself 'beggars', were hanging around the already bustling market. All were hoping for a day's work for a miserly reward that came their way, but he lost out at the market. He rushed to the seafront and busy harbour to see if there were any odd jobs available. However, without a home-made wooden cart and unwilling to tote loads on his head because it resulted in bad headaches later, he wasn't lucky there either.

He didn't become downhearted though; he wandered around town begging for work. As the afternoon hurriedly rushed to its end and the shadows got longer, he became beaten down by the sheer paucity of his life. Weighed down with hunger and depression, he walked to the beach bordering Bay Street in front of the market and sat down on the still hot, dark sand. He wasn't sure how long he sat there; he was too tired of life to move when a hand touched his shoulder.

"Hey man, why you sitting on the hot sand? Hungry? Here!"

Leroy handed him a small loaf, a couple of pieces of black pudding, and a glass bottle of locally produced sweet drink. Earl took the meal and ate daintily as though he were a prim old lady eating in revered company. Leroy sat down next to him and ate his meal. He felt sorry for the young man, saw potential in him, and wanted to harness that ambition, but at that moment he feared for him.

A job for Slim

"Finished? Come, we go cut hair; follow me!"

"But, today is Friday," Earl said, confused.

"I know, it's Friday. Sometimes I come to town Friday and go to Murray Village and places around. Get up, let's go!" he commanded.

Earl slowly got up and walked with his future mentor towards Murray Village, a small hidden suburb just north-east of the town centre. Leroy explained that this was one of his haunts, cutting the hair of the different ethnicities that lived there. As they neared their destination, Earl began to feel better and felt grateful for the help and potential Leroy saw in him. In a small clearing in the middle of the settlement, people were already gathering.

Young men in loose groups liming and eyeing up the girls, teenage girls huddled together giggling, small children running around wildly happily playing, and older people chatting casually. As expected, they flocked to the barber, but only a few wanted haircuts and paid whatever they could afford, though Leroy made it clear it was twenty to thirty cents for a child's and up to a dollar for a full head of hair depending on condition and length.

Earl watched carefully as Leroy took the small wooden box from under his arm, laid it on the ground, and opened it to expose an array of hair-cutting instruments. He carefully observed the deft fingers flying smoothly around the customers' heads but was just as intrigued with his teacher's loquaciousness. Leroy talked incessantly to his avid audience about his life, his childhood, his long-suffering mother and her wayward brother, and the beautiful, isolated 'Mespo' valley. When it began to get too dark, the overhead lamppost giving inadequate light, the customers dried up.

Suddenly, a stooped, slightly disabled man with a crooked walking stick arrived and sat down on the stool. His name was Clarence, and without warning, Leroy thrust the tiny comb and the pair of scissors he was using into Earl's hands. The scissors felt unwieldy in his right hand, his long, skinny fingers slipping around inside the loops on the handle. The long tapering blades looked lethal; the thin comb felt flimsy and inadequate and slipped from his grasp repeatedly, dropping into the hair-strewn loose dirt.

"No, hold them like this!" Leroy ordered. He then demonstrated how to hold the tools of his trade properly, how to make them feel natural in the hands, and how to cut the hair evenly and effortlessly. Clarence looked nervous as Leroy roughly pushed his head to the side so that Earl could take his first snip at the greying, thinning, loosely curled hair. Leroy was a good teacher, and by the time they were finished, Earl was smiling, Leroy was relieved and Clarence was grateful to escape unscathed without so much as a nip.

Leroy stood back and watched as Earl swept up the strewn tufts of hair off the dusty earth in the little clearing they stood in. He heaped praise on the young man for his quick learning, and for the first time since moving to Kingstown, Earl had a spring in his step and high hopes for his future. Clarence winked at the men as he hobbled off. Earl caught Leroy's friendly nod and then understood why Clarence didn't pay for the haircut. Obviously, Leroy had arranged it all, Clarence didn't have to pay so long as he allowed Earl to practise on him. He was compliant because he liked Leroy and took to the polite but bedraggled young man. Being deprived in life and poverty had taught Clarence that everyone needed a break.

As they walked out of Murray Village, Leroy thrust twenty dollars into his pupil's hand, commanding him to go to his friend Winston, who had a small cramped store in lower Middle Street, to purchase a decent set of clothes, including shoes and a comb. Earl protested and tried to return the money that he felt he didn't earn; he told Leroy that he had fifteen dollars already saved up to do just that one day. Leroy insisted he kept the money, and when he is able to, he can pay him back one day. By the time he had his hair cut down almost to the scalp a week later, he was wearing a new pair of shiny cheap shoes, a light blue short-sleeved buttoned down shirt, a pair of dark trousers, and at last a comb and a long-desired toothbrush; luckily he had only lost a couple of molars.

It was slow in coming, but working with Leroy's a few days a week and still managing to get other piecemeal work around the town, Earl achieved his biggest improvement since his move to Kingstown. He acquired a room for himself in a rooming house up Sion Hill; he had an actual bed to lay his tired body down at night. He laughed at the black ants who dared come indoors to annoy him. He didn't have to share anything with them any more but didn't mind the long-legged brown spiders and small green lizards that invaded and behaved as though his new home was their own property. Flies were pesky intruders, and the persistent mosquitoes never bothered his sound sleep during the night.

Sion Hill wasn't far from Leroy's barbershop down in Arnos Vale, which was down a tiny dirt road off the main highway, which forked towards the east coast and also towards inland, terminating at Mesopotamia. He had tried to get a place in Bottom Town but was unsuccessful; however, the place up Sion Hill was infinitely better placed for him and his new working regime. He hated leaving Pearl behind; she had treated him like a son, and he cared for her immensely.

She didn't have any family, and Earl wanted her status to improve just like his. He tried in vain to encourage her to share his new home with him; he would sleep on the floor while she had the bed. Better than the rags she slept on in her hut, he reflected. But she said she was happy where she was and wished him well in his new life. She never wanted to leave the area she grew up in and where she felt comfortable, though it could be rowdy and downright dangerous sometimes.

Before he walked over to Arnos Vale to Leroy's every weekday, he would check his work tools. He would open his small wooden box to reveal a couple of tapered combs with wide teeth at one end and tiny, fine teeth at the other. He also had a long-handled clipper comb with wide teeth ideal for thick hair, a thin, long-bladed, sharp pair of scissors, a flat-backed brush, a shaving brush and cut-throat razor for the customers who trusted him to give them a shave. He had Leroy to thank for his tools and also for the opportunity to go further inland to earn a little extra.

One such place he chose to go to was Lower Lowmans on the western side of the island, just a mile or so from Kingstown, because he knew someone who lived there. A lady called Evangeline, whom he got to know quite well at the market where she sold ground provisions and raw peanuts, asked him to cut her physically disabled father's and mentally disabled son's hairs. Evangeline used to cut her men's hair herself but had hurt her right hand while digging the ground up the mountain tending to her provisions that she would eventually sell in the market. She found it too painful to hold a pair of scissors properly and feared she would unintentionally cause damage to her men.

Earl soon found he was in great demand every time he went to Leeward to cut the Evangeline family's hair. She had advertised his adeptness with the scissors to all and sundry in and around her village, and to Earl's amazement, he found himself wandering, with his tool kit, around such places. He climbed steep hills, crossed fast-running streams and rivers, and fought off sandflies on dark sandy beaches near seaside settlements every weekend. Leroy was happy with his pupil's ambition, but the more confident Earl became, the more he wished to leave Leroy's employ and become independent.

The semi-illiterate tiny island boy was growing daily into an astute businessman with a good head for financial planning and future ideas. For over three years he worked with Leroy five days a week and on weekends went on his Leeward jaunts. His fortunes were changing, and for the first time he was making enough money to save a little, but he knew he was a long way from being affluent. But Earl's tenure at Leroy's was to end surprisingly abruptly.

Leroy's son Marvin returned from Aruba, where he had gone years earlier to make his fortune; he returned suddenly with an Aruban wife and a couple of small children. With a substantial amount of money in his pocket, he coaxed his father to expand into other ventures. He suggested that the barbershop, which was a room in the family home, should be turned into a grocery store, which he would manage. The barbershop would be located at the back of the shop, which his father should continue to run. He promised his parents that he would build a lovely house on the expanded plot near the shop large enough for all of them.

Leroy thought his son's ideas were brilliant and, as he was 'getting on', was happy to place everything into his son's capable hands. Earl was forced to re-evaluate his options; he felt an instant dislike towards Marvin, whom he could see didn't want him to be a part of the family business. He suspected Marvin was devious and no comparison to his jolly, trustworthy, easy-going father or supportive mother, Gloria. However, he could see that a small grocery store would be welcomed in an area growing in popularity but which had only a few amenities. He thought it a very good idea, though he'd never dreamt of voicing that to the cocky Marvin, whom he felt looked at him as an uneducated fool hanging on to his benevolent parents.

Earl knew his days were numbered at Leroy's and was heartbroken that he had to bid farewell to a friend that believed in him and his potential from the start. He had decided once he had discovered lush, laid-back Leeward, that was where his future lay. Leroy understood and embraced Earl's slight frame on the day they parted company, and Gloria said she was sad to see him go and begged him to visit them as often as possible. Marvin flashed a sly smile, confirming Earl's fear that he wanted him out of the family business.

Leeward

"OK, Slim, good luck in Leeward, and don't forget us," said Leroy with glistening, watery eyes as Earl walked away from Arnos Vale for good.

There were already a couple of well-established barbershops in Kingstown, so it made sense to go to the poorer but burgeoning far country, Leeward-side, on the west side of the island. Over time, the more he travelled there cutting hair, the more he got to know and appreciate the area and people better. He went to Bottom Town to beg Pearl to move with him to Leeward once he got settled there. But Pearl, born and bred in Bottom Town and having never ever visited any other part of her small island outside the capital, had never heard of a place called Buccament Bay where Earl said he was going to live, maybe permanently.

She was concerned that it would be too underdeveloped and said she heard that some people still lived in mud huts and were not as civilised as the capital's residents. He laughed heartily and tried to update her backward thinking of the countryside beyond

Kingstown, but she still declined his offer. Buccament was indeed a tiny scattered settlement with a few ramshackle dwellings that stretched from close to the black-sanded seaside inwards and upwards into the surrounding hills.

Most people were indeed dirt poor, and some may even once have lived as Pearl presumed, but things had moved on considerably by the dawn of the 1960s. In mileage, Kingstown was just 'down the road' from these small settlements and villages. However, because of little or no public transport, the high meandering steepness of the terrain and poor roads, the inhabitants of the capital were reluctant to travel inland to explore their beautiful, verdant and heavily forested homeland.

On the other hand, some country people were obliged to make regular trips to the capital for a host of reasons: secondary education, work, medical treatment, collecting merchandise and government business, such as paying taxes. Most people walked up and down the steep road that connected Leeward to the capital. If they could afford it as Earl did on some occasions, they used the infrequent large wooden cumbersome but gaudily painted passenger buses that rocked precariously as they travelled on the narrow, twisty highway.

He chose to live there because he loved the sheer fresh lushness all around and, as he remembered, it was far removed from the low, sparsely wooded Mayron with only its wide, flat silver beaches to give it character. He also, for the first time in his life, met a lovely lady with the most beautiful smile that stirred him deeply. He hoped he could marry her one day.

At first in Buccament, the twenty-seven-year-old boarded with a family who lived just off the beach and quite close to the river flowing through the settlement to the sea. He slept on a thin horsehair mattress on a narrow-wire framed bed crammed into a tiny back room. Earl was comfortable living there, even though at night he felt every knot in the wire under him, sticking into his thin frame. There wasn't a proper barbershop anywhere close, but he was aware that local people, men and women alike, cut the hair of family and friends, and some were very good at it. He travelled around Leeward to ply his trade, and soon he was a common sight in Questelles, Chauncey, Clare Valley and other remote scattered settlements inland.

Over time, people got used to seeing him with his wooden box, containing the tools of his trade, under his arm and a stool in the other hand. It was hard graft making money; he had to charge the barest minimum, and sometimes he would cut the odd child's hair for provisions or fruit. He walked everywhere wearing out his one pair of shoes. Eventually, his hard work and diligence paid off. Samuel, a well-known elderly man who once ran a tiny shop just off the beach, mainly selling home-made food, home-made soft drinks and rum, which some referred to as the 'rum shop on the beach', was selling up to move on. After years of toiling, getting old and tired, and the death of his wife, he decided to leave Buccament and move back to where he had originally come from, Chateaubelair, a small village further up the coast not far from the island's sleeping volcano.

Earl saw the rudimentary sign nailed to the rough door and wondered if he could afford to buy the property and turn it into a proper barbershop. He scratched his head with the frustration of someone who wanted to improve but didn't know how to. He passed the premises every day dreaming of a miracle, then one Sunday, as he exited the sea after a long refreshing swim in the deep waters off Buccament Bay, Samuel cornered him on the beach for a chat.

He offered the young man the shop – well, the whole of the

tiny building which consisted of only two rooms – the shop in the front and a back room. It was a bit rickety, but it had given him and his wife a better than average living in that poor enclave they domiciled in. Samuel wasn't being magnanimous; he was being crafty because he wanted out, and as nobody seemed interested in buying his now empty old home, he was willing to drop the price and push it onto the only businessperson in the area who seemed eager to own something.

Lightly tapping Earl's chest in encouragement, Samuel lauded the importance of owning one's own business while encouraging Earl to buy. He could see the young man's tight facial muscles change showing interest, so he talked him into going to a small family run bank in town and hoped they would help Earl as they did years before with him.

"Look, Slim, ah give you the shop for two hundred dollars," he said. "Try, boy, you have a good head for business."

"Ah hear about them from me good friend Leroy; ah'll try me luck," replied the upbeat young man.

"Don't hang about; plenty of people interested!" The crafty old man lied.

Earl looked around the two empty rooms and couldn't stop smiling because every step he made confirmed in him a feeling of hope of better things to come. Before he went to bed that night, he removed a small tin from under his mattress, opened it and counted out his savings – eighty dollars, much of it in change. He shook his head at his meagre savings, realising it would take him years to save up two hundred dollars. He realised to get anywhere with his plans he would need to borrow a substantial amount of money.

That night he was too discomfited to sleep, and the thin mattress with the lacerating wire underneath didn't bother him one bit. Every second awake was spent mulling over the things he would say to the people at the bank and how he would conduct his new business on the beach. He pushed aside thoughts of failure that kept invading his anxious mind.

As he sat down in front of the older, stern-faced, balding but elegantly suited man who was sitting behind a large mahogany desk, Earl lost all confidence. He had never before spoken to or even been in the same room as such a person, and he became afraid. He rose from the leather chair about to leave when the realisation hit him that someone like him could never understand the language or the nuances of running a business from the man in front of him who was so far removed from his sphere.

"Sit down, sir," said the man, breaking into a friendly smile. "How can I help you?"

"Sorry, sir, ah think ah waste your time, sorry for bothering you," Earl said visibly, trembling as he rose to his feet to flee the building.

The gentleman was more amenable than he had expected and encouraged him to sit down and explain why he came to the bank in the first place. With a timorous, barely audible voice, Earl related his whole life story and outlined the plan for his future that he only had managed to save eighty dollars so far and was hoping for a chance to improve, but he didn't want to waste the banker's time.

He couldn't give any guarantees that his business would be successful, especially as he was only a small-time barber. It looked like his plan was a non-starter; a flash of his future looked like years of travelling around Leeward, hawking for business. After all, he thought grimly, who would give a loan to an unschooled, homeless man? No one but a fool, and the man in front of him was no such thing. He bowed his head in defeat, but he perked up when he realised he was being listened to ardently.

The smart 'money-man' asked him to come back in a week for a decision and to deposit his savings in the bank, where it would be much safer than under a mattress. So after depositing the fifty dollars to start a savings account in a bona fide bank for the first time in his life, he left the building with a little bank book and feeling more upbeat than when he had entered.

When he got back to Buccament, he reported to Samuel that he had to return to the bank the following week for a decision. Samuel said that that was a good sign. A week later, he got his loan; he was given two hundred dollars, the full amount he asked for. After explanations and promises about repayments, he scratchily signed a lot of papers, mostly which he couldn't read or understand, and left the bank walking on air.

Earl was the happiest man on earth when he handed over the crisp one hundred and fifty dollars to Samuel after beating him down from the two hundred dollars he was asking for, which everyone had said was too much for the 'shack' anyway. The newly acquired property was extensively repaired; a thick coat of blue-green paint was daubed carefully on the wooden exterior while light-brown paint adorned the inside.

The shop space was large enough for the proper, though old-fashioned, barber chair, which was a gift from Leroy. There was also a small table on which rested an enamel ewer and basin, and a couple of smoothed-down brown painted wooden chairs filled the rest of the shop space. In the room behind was the living area, just large enough for a single bed and a narrow bedside table. The front door faced the usually calm sea, of which the low waves silently and gently crept up the black-sand beach, mesmerising the coastal residents and beach visitors alike with its sluggishness.

This little place, which was cooled by a steady south-westerly breeze, became quite quickly a popular hub of activity, especially in the evenings and all-day Saturdays. Earl was astute in charging his customers according to their ability to pay rather than going by a set price. People heard of his new seaside shop through word of mouth and came from inland and around coastal areas to avail themselves of his expertise and friendliness.

Before in Kingstown, he was a hungry, silent man who said very little and would speak only when spoken to. Some had said he was a bit retarded and stayed well away from him, unsure whether he would be prone to violence. But by observing Leroy's relationship with his customers, he learnt to reinvent himself and gradually fostered a friendlier, more welcoming demeanour. Therefore, to help build his business and make a little money, he became a man of tales, real and imagined, and had his customers and curious visitors agog with his knowledge and skill as a raconteur.

Everyone became familiar with the adventures of 'Slim' and his mentor Leroy. His tall tales kept the customers intrigued and returning for more. Mayron, his once long-forgotten birthplace, became a mythical place full of sea tales of daring adventures of whalers, pirates and pleasure seekers. He told his audience that the few people who lived scattered on that tiny bit of land in the Caribbean Sea hailed it as a magical place where dreams always came true. He could make up stories with such ease that he surprised himself that ideas came thick and fast whenever there was an eager listener in front of him.

But he did have quiet moments, especially when most people were out grafting a living and at lunch times. His girlfriend, Hannah, would bring him lunch, tasty meals of rice and peas accompanied with freshly caught boiled or fried fish, saltfish and breadfruit, crayfish from the nearby river or ground-provisions, and vegetables flavoured with callaloo. They would both eat while sitting outside the shop on the wooden chairs or cooped up inside if it was raining or too windy. He wasn't fussy about what he ate and enjoyed each meal with the same relish he did when he shared Pearl's meagre offerings.

No one was as happy and content as Earl, even when he had to pay money back to the bank every month, taxes and other expenses for the first time in his life. He wasn't aware people paid taxes until the time he accompanied Leroy to the tax office in town. He was amazed that taxes had to be paid for almost everything, such as homes, the land they stood on, businesses, whether small or large, and that wages were also taxable.

He learnt about water and electricity bills when Pearl said she was glad she didn't have to bother about any of that. She had overheard Mrs Ryan, who owned the grocery store on the corner, complaining to a customer about all the money she spent on such things. Pearl collected water in a bucket from the public standpipe near her home and used a kerosene lamp when she could afford to buy kerosene or candles for lighting. Earl, like most of his neighbours, was doing the same, collecting water from a standpipe nearby.

Customers rarely stayed around when it got dark, but a few local men 'hung' around to 'lime' after dark when a nip of rum would liven the atmosphere. On those evenings he would light a lantern and hang it from a nail above the front door; it gave ample light, which all the beachside residents took advantage of on the rare dark moonless nights.

Hannah Makes Two

"Hannah, we should get married," he said unexpectedly one day to Hannah.

He was getting worried that if he didn't make it official with this eligible lady soon, he'd lose her for good. Though she didn't have higher schooling, she was clever and literate, and he depended on her to help him with the official part of running the business. He was flummoxed by all the government paperwork and keeping the 'books' for the business, so he needed someone articulate to explain things properly to him.

"When I fix it up with my father so that we can live with him, we'll get married!" Hannah replied in a casual manner, impressing her fiance with a slightly uppity accent and articulate speech.

Hannah knew they couldn't afford much and hoped her father, Alvin Howe, a hard-working, no-nonsense country man with rough hands and a sparsely unruly beard, would allow them to share his home. The wooden grey-slatted, rough-looking two-bedroom house, which was a bit inland from the bay and up above the main road, was her home since birth.

She was effectively her father's housekeeper ever since her mother died years ago, when she was barely into her teens. After her mother's passing, she was too young to go off looking for work, but when she was only fourteen years of age, her mother's sister, Olga, found her some shop work not too far away in Questelles, where she lived. A wealthy couple named Talman owned a large store merchandising in food and dry goods, which they administered with the help of various assistants and sometimes, their children.

By the time Hannah was taken on, Mr Talman had died and

his older son and daughter had moved overseas; the business was diminishing due to more competition, and the elderly Mrs Talman was struggling with it after a stroke. Her youngest daughter was a civil servant in Kingstown and only came home on weekends and appeared to show no interest in the store. Hannah was very good at her job and willingly helped the ageing lady, who at first was not sure if she could trust Hannah, sat obsessively by the cash register guarding her money.

However, she soon realised that the girl had an astute brain and could calculate money with lightning speed. She would accurately call out the tab's total and how much change, if any, to return to the customer before Mrs Talman even opened the money drawer. Mrs Talman eventually began to like Hannah a little too much for her jealous daughter's liking because her mother talked about her teenage assistant incessantly and with greater softness each day. Hannah, in turn, had taken to Mrs Talman like a mother, whom she would do anything for and more.

Sometimes Mrs Talman would ask her to close up the premises during the lunch hour so that the two of them could sit together and eat lunch, which was prepared by her maid, without interruption. Both enjoyed those moments immensely, each wishing the other was her relative, but the jealous servant relayed these encounters to Mrs Talman's daughter, who, on the rare occasions, saw Hannah would flash her a sour look. Unfortunately, it all came crashing down for Hannah not long after she turned eighteen. The fragile Mrs Talman died in her sleep, and Hannah became redundant; the lady's daughter sold up the business and family home and moved to the capital to live permanently. The new shop owners didn't require Hannah's help, and so she returned to her father unemployed and depressed.

Alvin, fearing for her safety so far from his watchful eyes if she moved to the capital for work, knew it was only a matter of time his daughter would leave home. One Sunday, when she and some friends lazily lounged on Buccament Bay beach, she met the enigmatic barber. Alvin didn't mind at all because, though Earl wasn't from their area, he was a countryman at heart and hopefully would stay in Leeward forever. So he agreed to the young couple living with him after their marriage, but he was hoping Earl would do some repairs before the big day. He decided to have a heart to heart with his prospective son-in-law. Like most of the men around, he had heard the stories, but unlike most, he took everything Earl said with a pinch of salt.

Nearly a year later, and after the canny young man saw the potential in expanding his little shop, he began selling hair and beauty products as well as doing the barber work. This meant customers would not have the extra expense of going to the capital just to buy hair products such as oils, pomades, combs, brushes, clips, pins or even ribbons for little girls' hairs. So, from a man in Middle Street who acquired these items legally from imported freight, he bought stuff to resell to his customers.

Soon adorning a couple of hastily built shelves were a variety of hair products to keep the tight curls of hair loose and manageable and beauty products such as talcum powder, face powder, body lotion, nail varnish and blood-red lipstick. Customers came from near and far to view or to buy, even when they didn't need a haircut.

One morning, not long after he opened his shop, Alvin greeted Earl, "Marnin' Slim!"

"Good morning, Mr Alvin; you come for a trim, a shave. Sit down, please," he said pleasantly, pointing to the barber chair.

"Ah don't come for a haircut or shave. Ah want to talk to

you." His voice was humourless, and Earl lost his confident air. He sat down, waiting for whatever Alvin was going to talk about.

"Did ah do something wrong, sir?" he asked in a tiny voice.

"Oh, shut up and listen!" Alvin was a serious man and was not the sort of man you crossed; he would kill any man who wronged his only child.

"Yes, sir!" Earl waited to hear what he did wrong.

"Ah know you love Hannah and want to marry her; I agree, but she say you want to live in MY house." His eyes critically perused Earl's tiny place, then he sat down on the other chair.

"Only temporary, cause this is too small," Earl said meekly, waving his hand as though he were showing Alvin the place for the first time.

"Just listen!" Alvin ordered.

Then he pointed out that Earl could clearly see that his place was too small for the couple to live in comfortably and expressed sadness for poor Etta, Samuel's wife, who had to squeeze in with that cantankerous fool till death released her. Anyhow, he continued, in order for the couple to live with him, the house would have to be repaired. There was a leaky roof and rotten floor boards to be replaced, and a splash of paint would upgrade the place ready for them after they were married. The sooner, the better he suggested.

Earl was stunned; he expected worse. Poor Alvin, being kind and attentive to Hannah, couldn't afford to repair his rotting home. He did his best with repairs but knew it needed radical upgrading. He earned very little selling his mountain produce and, unknown to Hannah, spent a lot of time worrying about their predicament.

When Hannah was employed, she used to give her father most of her wages, just keeping a bit for herself for her personal care, but they never had enough to save. She was happy to move to the capital to look for work, but he forbade it, too frightened he would lose her for good. She was an adult and could have left any time to try to improve their lot but didn't want to upset her doting father so stayed by his side and kept house for them both. The men sat and chatted for a while about what could be done, then Alvin shook Earl's hand and left. He went home to collect his cutlass, hoe and rake before going uphill to tend his mountain plot. He was glad Hannah had found a good man whom he was sure would be as kind to her as he was to her mother.

Some weeks later, Earl did not open the shop as usual. The few prospective customers who came along read a large handwritten notice that said 'closed today'. Everyone wanted to know what was going on, and one man even went up the hill to ask Hannah and Alvin what was going on, but they pretended they had no idea what Earl was up to. Earl arrived back on the late afternoon bus and was met by Hannah and Alvin at the roadside below their home. They unloaded a vast amount of merchandise, which curious onlookers could see were for house repairs. Planks of wood, sheets of galvanise for the roof, cans of paint, bags of nails, putty and cement. The trio lugged the goods up the hill, and no one was happier than Alvin, who couldn't wait to start with the renovations. Earl promised he would help Alvin on his slack days, which were quite a few except his best work day, Saturdays.

Earl had never worked so hard in his life but had done building work and carpentry before when he and others repaired his beachside shack. All three of them sawed, hammered, painted and slogged to make the place look nice, and when it was finished, it certainly did look immaculate with its freshly painted interior and exterior. The little house stood out bright and proud on the hillside as though it were newly built. Unfortunately, their magnificent effort of improvement made all their neighbours' homes look dismal and ramshackle.

Earl was happy when the work on the house was finished; he needed to get back to making money in order to pay back the extra loan he borrowed. It wasn't much, but it was a huge amount for his small business to recoup. He needed enough for the repairs, for the business and to finance his forthcoming wedding. Life moved another step forward when he and Hannah married a few months later.

The wedding took place in a little Methodist church in Questelles village on a drizzly Saturday afternoon. The reception afterwards was in the village hall almost smack on the highway, advertising the event to all and sundry. There was plenty of home-made food, the popular Pelau rice dish, spicy crayfish callaloo soup, the traditional 'Black' cake, and plenty of beer and sweetened home-made drinks. A West Indian party won't be anything without rum; it was a necessity, so there were bottles of rediculously strong white rum and several milder varieties of dark rum to choose from.

The calypso music, mostly featuring The Mighty Sparrow, a Trinidadian legend, was played at an ear-splittingly loud volume on a hi-fi belonging to one of Earl's many Buccament Bay 'friends', the fun-loving Noah Sims. The musical sounds could be heard right across the valley and attracted a lot of uninvited 'guests' all vying for a bit of the action and insisting they were Slim's best friends. Long after the bride and groom went home, the festivities continued until around ten o'clock, when Alvin called time and broke up the merriment. By then, only the drunken men and fresh sagaboys were left misbehaving, physically rumbustious and screamingly loud that Alvin had no option but to break up the party to prevent breakages and expenditure. When it was all over, he sighed with relief, then he entered his sister-in-law's home, where he would stay for a night in order to give the married couple at least one night of privacy.

The couple, living with Alvin, continued with their everyday lives. Earl did his job cutting hair, while Hannah, because she had the experience, helped her husband as much as possible in the rapidly increasing business, plus she tended the house for the men in her life. Sometime later, when she announced she was 'expecting', her husband was spurred to upgrade further. Luckily, his business was doing really well, not only with his barber work but more so with the retail side, where there was little spare space in the front and the back room was cramped floor to ceiling with merchandise. He became concerned over the lack of space and the poor security in the tin shack building.

He heard of and eventually saw an empty two-storey building in Layou just waiting for someone to take the financial risk and hopefully make good money in the fast-growing seaside village not too far from Buccament Bay. He went back to the bank and confidently asked for a small, manageable mortgage on the bigger premises. He impressed the mortgage lenders so much with his successful business acumen that he managed to obtain a mortgage of many years duration.

Layou mirrored Kingstown in a way that it lay on a flat area in front of a natural bay, gradually rising into the hills surrounding it. It was laid out similarly to the capital, with three parallel streets running east to west with business and residential properties lining the thoroughfares. The building he acquired consisted of ample shop space on the ground floor and spacious living quarters upstairs. It had previously belonged to a family who ran a general store for many years, but old age and death intervened, and the shop lay empty for several years, waiting for someone brave enough to return it to a profitable business.

Alvin was sad to see the couple leave, not only for company, but his homemaker Hannah would no longer be there to cook, clean and wash his earth-encrusted work clothes. He pretended to be easy about their decision and wished the couple a good life. Earl advised him to get a lodger or rent the house and move with them to Layou; it was a short distance from Buccament. He didn't want to leave his home and didn't want to rent it out to strangers, who might destroy the place. He preferred solitude, he lied, but would always be there if his daughter or her husband needed him.

The last time Earl saw Leroy was at the wedding; he invited him over to the opening of his new shop. Leroy was impressed with the young man's ambition and praised him for moving upwards so quickly. The two men talked of the future, and he was grateful for the break Leroy had given him; he was moving forward and upwards faster than either of them ever imagined. Leroy felt redundant, but Marvin had done everything he said he would; a new and highly profitable grocery store, a new barbershop and a new house for the family.

At first, Leroy was lord of his domain, but slowly Marvin took over, sidelining his father, eventually forcing him into retirement. Foundering and increasingly bored, he continued freelance barbering in and around Kingstown, only for that to end abruptly when a stroke affected his sight and weakened his right hand.

He walked around the shop, nodding his head at the merchandise, especially the ones for personal care and beauty. He loved the whiff of sweetness permeating the air from the tiny bottles of scents and ran his slightly numb hand along the smooth varnished counter. He sat in the brand-new barber chair in the room adjoining the shop and smiled when he saw the tools of the trade neatly arranged on a side table. He was so proud of Earl and wished he was his son, but immediately felt guilty for thinking badly of his son, who had increased the family fortune considerably.

"Slim, you done well, boy." He smiled and slapped the thin shoulders. "Hope you didn't overstretch yourself to get all this."

"Ah got a big mortgage; it will take me years to pay it back. Ah believe profit in this." Earl waved his arms around with a flourish.

"You right, young man, banks would never back a loser, I think they see you're a man with prospects."

"One day I'll pay it all back!" His thin face lit up with the smile of a confident successful businessman.

He worked harder than ever, cutting hair from morning till night. At first, Hannah ran the shop, but after she had their first child, she found it exhausting being a housewife, mother, bookkeeper and shop assistant, Earl decided to take on an assistant. Netty, a teenage girl, sat on most days of the week with her mother a few doors down from the shop, selling peanuts, coconut delicacies and tamarind balls from a large wooden tray. She wished for better and spent a lot of time trying to talk her mother into going to the capital to sell in the market. Her mother didn't think they would be any better off with so much more competition in town; Netty felt trapped. Every day she saw what was going on in Earl and Hannah's world and wished some of that good fortune would come her way.

She walked into the shop one day to see if she could afford some perfume or maybe a small jar of cold cream, but at a glance, she could see everything was too expensive for her. She didn't know where it came from, but as she was leaving the shop, she turned to the seated Hannah with her baby in her arms and, pronouncing her words as clearly as possible, said, "Morning, Mrs Drake, have you got work? Anything! I can cook, clean, wash, sell, whatever you want doing!"

Hannah knew the girl, seeing her every day, and felt sorry for her but shook her head regrettably. She wished she could help all the desperate people around her because she knew their stories, once hers as well. She suggested to her husband that they take on someone to help her in the shop. He agreed that they needed help and said he had someone in mind already. Hannah smiled, being sure it would be Netty. However, she was taken aback when he gleefully told her that he had taken on a young man to train as a barber and help in the shop.

The new assistant was a teenage boy about Netty's age called Joel, whose family lived in an inland settlement called Vermont and who were Alvin's friends. His poor family wanted him to do something better than backbreaking menial landwork. They had a word with Alvin, who encouraged his son-in-law to give the young man a break. Joel was happy to get out of tiny Vermont, so he enthusiastically accepted the position to train to be a barber. He viewed Layou as a prosperous little town miles better than puny Vermont; he had never been to Kingstown, and Earl wondered how he would react to the bigger and more developed capital if he thought Layou was a bustling metropolis.

Hannah, who never argued needlessly with her husband, was heartbroken for Netty and hoped she would get something better to do than sitting all day behind a wooden tray waiting hopefully for a sale. So many others were doing the same, vying for the few customers willing to spend on a titbit they could ill afford themselves. It was when Hannah was heavily pregnant with her second child more than a year later that Netty was taken on to help the couple. She was so glad to work indoors that she didn't care what she did; she cooked, cleaned, washed clothes, ironed, did childminding and helped from time to time in the shop.

With a good marriage and a thriving business, Earl was at his most content, and during all that time he never thought of his friends from back home on Mayron. So, it was a total shock when he bumped into Verna one Sunday afternoon in Kingstown. He wasn't honest with Verna though, mischievously misleading her by failing to tell her about Hannah and his children. He was astonished that a young lady of her calibre was working as a maid, but she had said she was hoping for better.

After his initial shock, he was enthralled by her beauty, noting how tall, graceful and well-spoken she was – not the little timid girl he last saw back home. He was filled with regrets for laughing at Mayron and ignoring his friends. He told Hannah of his meeting with Verna and how sorry he was that she couldn't get to do something better than domestic work and said he wanted to help. But Hannah forbade him interfering in things that don't concern them and felt Verna was capable of making her own dreams come true.

The months flew by, and Earl was too busy with his own life to waste time thinking about Verna or Mayron and therefore put them all firmly out of his mind. He worked tirelessly, craving success, and never thought that he would be happily married with children and be the owner of a thriving business with employees. He even bought a second-hand family car that only Joel could drive; he had taken driving lessons but found it too technical and stressful, so he gave up. Young Joel, being the legal age to drive, was eager to learn and soon became Earl's chauffeur.

Pearl and Rudolf

On one of his monthly trips to the capital to pay bills and taxes, he went down as usual to Bottom Town to check on his old friend, Pearl. He found her tiny home empty but didn't have to ask where she was because almost immediately her equally elderly neighbour Des'ree called out to him, letting him know Pearl was in the hospital. He didn't waste time asking questions; he rushed to the hospital nearby and soon found her in the female ward. Asking permission from the sister to see his friend though it wasn't visiting time, he was granted but was told she was very ill and may not survive the day.

He sat at her side, shocked that she had deteriorated so quickly after seemingly being well when he saw her only a few weeks before. Somehow, she didn't look sick or haggard but looked as though she was in a peaceful sleep, breathing quietly. He held her hand and was amazed by its softness. He wasn't sure how long he sat in the curtained-off area down the end of the ward but reluctantly had to move to allow the nurses to attend to the dying woman. He stood outside the ward just at the top of the stairs of the first-floor ward, waiting to go back to his friend when he was called into the ward sister's office.

She asked him what relation he was to Pearl and when the time came if he would be paying for her funeral or would it be a pauper's grave. This shook Earl up a lot when the distant memory of his poor mother's demise flooded his memory. But he informed the nurse that he was not a blood relative but did live with her years ago before he moved to Leeward, then he assured the no-nonsense lady that he would see to all of the expenses because he wanted his dear friend to have a good send-off.

"When last did you see Miss Potter?" asked the sister, whose slimness rivalled his.

"Three weeks ago, maybe. Ah didn't know she was so sick so fast; nobody told me. Pearl was my mother, here!" He placed a hand over his heart, and tears dropped from his reddening eyes. He was surprised to know that her surname was Potter; no one ever used it in front of him, and it never occurred to him to ask her what her full name was, but she knew he was Earl Drake and not just 'Slim'. Not sure when the end would come, Earl returned home and broke the upsetting news to Hannah.

He had taken her to meet Pearl before their marriage, and the two women liked each other instantly. Hannah encouraged her husband to buy Pearl a bed and a small kerosene stove, which meant she didn't have to sleep on rags any more or to struggle to light a coal pot every day with kindling and coals before putting a pan of water on to make herself some bush tea of some sort. Pearl looked forward to his monthly visits when he came to town to do business. Usually he would bring a bag full of provisions and always put a dollar or two in her hand. Mostly, he would ask her for the umpteenth time to relocate to his part of the world, but she refused to abandon her run-down community and the many friends she had there since childhood.

The nursing sister was right; Pearl didn't last the day; she passed away just before midnight. Earl knew even before he arrived the next morning that she may already be in the mortuary. He was sent to the hospital office, where he was given a death certificate and directed to go to the registry office, which was in a large official building in town, to register the death. He was out of his depth and fumbled with the papers, not knowing how to conduct himself. Joel stayed close to him and helped him, but he needn't have worried about how to plan and effectuate a funeral. Pearl's landlord and other people who knew her got to work doing everything for the lady they knew, referring to her as 'good' Pearl. All grateful Earl had to do was pay for it all: the coffin, the service, the burial and the 'wake' afterwards.

 Joel drove Earl and Hannah back to town for the funeral, which would take place in the afternoon the day after she died. He dropped the couple off by the bottom of Nine Steps, where a large crowd waited to walk with Pearl to the church, then the cemetery. Earl got a lot of gentle pats and whispered 'Slim, God bless', as they walked to the open coffin outside her home, where Pearl seemed to be resting peacefully. A couple of large tubs of ice were placed under her coffin, keeping her cool in the searing tropical heat.

 After the large funeral, which looked like the whole of Bottom Town attended, the wake around her little home was in full swing. People were laughing and singing the praises of Pearl as people usually do after funerals, but only everything they said of Pearl was true. She was indeed a good soul that life was not kind to; born in poverty, lumbered with poor health, which interrupted her schooling and forced her to live in the worst possible conditions through lack of money and family to care for her.

 A week later, Joel dropped Earl off at the cemetery gates. He walked to the grave not too far inside the cemetery, removed some dead flowers, and then placed a bouquet of fresh flowers he brought with him in the middle of the heaped mound. He stood back looking at the grave and thinking over the times he shared with Pearl, how they talked about his improvised life and how she encouraged him to keep fighting to better himself and not give up like so many others had done and spent their lives begging or theiving.

 He became aware of someone close to him, turned and saw

a stylishly dressed old man with a large-brimmed felt hat pulled low over his forehead, smiling at him. He nodded at the newcomer but was a little annoyed that his reverie was interrupted. He began to walk away to meet Joel in Middle Street, where his business friend lived and worked, when the man stopped him.

"Morning, sir. Are you Mr Slim?"

"Yes, that's me, who wants to know," replied Earl, hoping it wasn't somebody looking for a handout, but the man in front of him was smart in appearance, which said he wasn't a beggar. The man offered his hand and said he was Pearl's cousin, Rudolf. Earl ignored the hand; sure that was a lie because she had told him many times that she had no one, not one single relative, but the man insisted he was related to Pearl. Earl hurriedly walked off, fearing that the man was definitely looking for a handout, word must have gotten around that he was a successful businessman and had paid for Pearl's funeral.

Rudolf hurried towards the departing Earl as he picked up stride and cried out, "I tell the truth, sir, Pearl and I are cousins."

Earl stopped, nodded to the man that he wanted to hear his sorry tale after all. Rudolf proceeded to tell the tale as they walked slowly to Earl's friend in Middle Street. He said that his mother and Pearl's mother were sisters with the same father but different mothers. They never knew each other existed, though one lived north of the town in Largo Height, while the other was born and bred in Rose Place within the town. The girls' obnoxious father abandoned their mothers and moved to Trinidad, where he eventually got married and had other children.

"But how do you know this is true?" asked Earl, really curious about this new development.

Soon they were crossing the bridge in Back Street, both men walking on the sidewalk towards the market and subsequently Earl's destination. Rudolf continued his tale that he suspected their mothers knew about each other because on her deathbed, his mother said he should look for relatives down in Kingstown but didn't make it clear who they were or where they lived. After her death, he did ask her friends if they knew anything about her family, but no one could help; overtime, he forgot all about it.

Rudolf, who was about Pearl's age, said that one day some months ago, a young Trinidadian man named Julian came to his house to inform him that he was his great-nephew. He was staggered and disputed Julian's claim, but the young man said that his grandmother, who would have been Rudolf's and Pearl's half-sister, told his mother that her long-dead father Theopholus was a Vincentian and that she was certain he said he had a couple of daughters in a place called Largo Height near Kingstown.

The young man said his mother was told this story many years ago, but she had never followed it up until recently, when she disclosed the family secret to him. Julian had researched the story well and went straight to Largo Height, where, after a few more inquiries, he arrived at Rudolf's door. The next thing was to find the other abandoned child's offspring, but when they found the connection, it was too late; she had passed away. When the two men were close to Earl's destination, Rudolf stopped and tottered, swaying from side to side.

Earl supported him and walked him gently to his friend's place nearby. They sat the old man down and gave him some water, but suspecting he may also be hungry, Earl's friend, Harry, retreated further into his small store to find something for the old man to eat. After eating a small crusty loaf and a piece of jackfish, Rudolf recovered and apologised for causing so much trouble.

"It's 'Sugar'," he said. "I should've eaten something; I forget sometimes."

The two men, now joined by Joel, said helping him was no big deal but advised him that he shouldn't be walking about in the hot sun at his age on an empty stomach. He stood up to leave, whereupon Earl offered him a lift to his home. He accepted, realising the long walk back in the boiling sun might be too much for him after all.

"So you have diabetes?" asked Harry.

"So the doctor says, but if I don't get hungry and eat less sugar, I am all right. No tablets at all. I'm OK, old but good!"

Joel brought the car to the store's door, Earl took his usual place in the back seat behind the driver, and Rudolf sat in front next to Joel. The car drove through the town centre, towards the west end of the capital, then turned north towards Leeward. The car seemed to be labouring packed with merchandise for the store safely in the boot, Joel confidently at the wheel.

"Am grateful for the lift; my legs are weak today. Drop me off by the 'Gardens', Mr Slim, I'll make my way home from there."

"Don't worry, Mr Rudolf, we take you home; just show Joel the way. My name is Earl, but for some reason, people call me Slim," said the thin man, warming to Pearl's cousin and wanting to see how he lived. "Is your nephew still over here?"

"No, no, he went back to Trinidad, but he's coming back in a few months; he said he doesn't want to lose his Vincentian connection. I like him; he's an electrician, got a wife, a child, a car and his own home. He's doing well; the whole Trini family is doing well," said Rudolf proudly.

Joel nervously was trying to manoeuvre the car further inland on a road getting narrower and more uneven, eventually stopping when the road became a narrow track. They stopped not far from a large, dazzling white single-storey wooden house with a wide veranda with an ornate balustrade dominating the front of the house and with a rocking chair all alone near the front door.

"That's my home; come in for a drink before you take the Leeward Road, Slim, and you too, Joel," said Rudolf, exiting the car.

"Thank you, sir, but we must be getting back now," said Earl. "Your wife must be waiting for you."

"Wife, no sir, no wife. Like Pearl, I never got hitched and no children either; it just never happened. See that house" – he pointed to the white house – "I built it for my mother, but she died before we moved in, so now I live there all alone. My mother was a good, gentle woman; she taught at a primary school down in the town for years, right up to retirement. She paid for me to go to grammar school, then to university. I wish we knew Pearl; we would've helped her. I gather she died in poverty. So sad!"

"Yes, sir, ah wish she knew she had family and in Trinidad too; she would've been really happy. She always said she's the only one in the world," said Earl sadly.

"Yes, sad! You have a domestic to help you, sir?" enquired Joel.

"Yes, my boy, she cooks, cleans, washes and irons my clothes; in fact, she looks after me like she's the wife" – he gave a cheeky titter – "but she lives elsewhere; no one else but me sleeps in my home."

Joel revved the car to signal they were leaving, but Rudolf hung on to the door and again begged them to come inside his white palace for refreshments. Earl politely smiled and shook his head, then Joel put the car into a slow reverse to turn around and leave Largo Height, but Rudolf was still blocking the way.

"I make things, you know, drawing room and dining room furniture, beds and all sorts; my workshop is over there." He pointed to a large garage-type workshop across the road where several men were assiduously toiling. "That's some of my staff. Next time you come to town, we can talk some more; get to know each other better."

"Have you always made furniture, Mr Rudolf?" Joel asked while still trying to turn the car around.

"No, young man, like my mother, I was a teacher. I taught English and English literature at a high school, but after about a decade I got bored and went into carpentry, much to my mother's annoyance. Surprisingly, I became successful and had to take on staff. Everyone said my furniture's the best, and we're still going strong," he said proudly.

Earl nodded and watched as the old man straightened his back, picked up his step, and marched towards his sparkling home, waving to his staff, who reciprocated, then returned to their work. The car and its occupants were soon back on the highway, pointed upwards and westwards towards Leeward.

"Look at that house, wow, it reeks of money, though I would have built it with bricks, not wood. Looks like he's very rich; bet he got land and plenty of rented properties as well. Miss Pearl would have been OK if she had known him," observed the usually silent Joel.

"Yes, she would."

"Will you visit him again, Mr Sim?"

"Yes, Pearl will like that," he said, as though she were alive and kicking. "Ah get a good feeling from him."

"True, I think he's the genuine thing. Imagine top education and a high school English teacher. I wonder where he went abroad to study. I wish I went to high school, then I'd go to uni too," said Joel. "You got another friend in town now, sir!"

Earl smiled and settled back in his seat, and as the car began to descend Lowman's Hill towards Questelles, the pain he felt losing Pearl suddenly lifted. He wanted to get home not just to tell Hannah the remarkable story of Pearl's new cousins she never knew existed, Rudolf in Largo Height and Julian the Trinidadian, but just to be with her and the children. He felt lucky having a family, having people around him, and for the first time in his life, he had truly banished the nagging loneliness of belonging nowhere that always haunted him. He had never felt so relaxed before, so sure of his continuing success and his wonderful family.

After one hard day's work and after he and his loved ones had eaten supper, he sat down alone on one of the strange low occasional plastic chairs Hannah acquired for their narrow first-floor balcony. He looked at the reddish-orange horizon, watching the sun fall away into the calm, darkening Caribbean Sea. The faintest outline of some Grenadine islands thrusted a painful memory upon his broad, thin shoulders. The once poor homeless boy had tears welling in his eyes as the spectre of his long-dead mother loomed large in front of him.

"Look, Mama, wish you can enjoy all this with us but ah know you are proud of me." He cocked his head to the left, listening intently; he was sure he heard Rosanna's tenuous voice saying, 'Good boy, Early, well done!'

Chapter 4

The Rich Lady

Arlene Cassocks' life continued in the vein it had always been prior to Verna's appearance. Every morning she and Sidney sat at a table full of an assortment of food: eggs, ham, fried plantain, home-made guava jelly, home-made orange marmalade and a large, partly sliced home-made loaf, with a pot of freshly brewed coffee amid fine porcelain. All professionally laid out on a white tablecloth bordered with lace on the highly polished six-chaired mahogany dining table with its thick ornate legs indicating class and wealth. After breakfast, she would decide if she wanted to check in on the family store down below in Port Elizabeth, go to the boatyard with Sidney, go to the yacht club to socialise with the other privileged wives, or just sit around the house mostly sipping cocktails or snoozing on the veranda on an expertly locally made low lounger.

Mostly though, after going for a long swim in the warm, calm sea at Lower Bay or the slightly rougher waters opposite the boatyard a little further east, she stayed at home doing absolutely nothing. Sometimes, because of the boredom, she upped and left Bequia for short breaks to see her family on the main island or visit distant family and friends in Barbados. Sidney became used to these trips because he knew she was bored with Bequia's quiet life. She was young in comparison to the other wives in her clique. She had spent many happy holidays in Bequia as a child and teenager, but she never dreamt she would marry a local or indeed live there permanently.

She was introduced to Sidney at a friend's party in St Vincent, then chose the handsome and wealthy young man from the Grenadians over the older Vincentian lawyer whom her family thought would make an ideal husband. Perhaps she was dreamy about the beautiful island she knew well from childhood, but after a short while there, boredom had set in. She spent a great deal of time fantasising because her greatest wish to have a child was not fulfilled. By the time she reached thirty, she had given up on ever having a baby and succumbed to the life of privilege and indulgence she was born into.

Verna was a naïve teenage girl when she came to work for the Cassocks, and at first, Arlene decided to have a little mischievous fun with her. She noted the youth and beauty of the girl and her willingness to please. The first time she spoke to Verna, she could tell the girl was not as uneducated as the others who worked for her. She noticed a sophistication in the young girl unseen in servants and a pleasing persona. She noted Verna was exceptionally beautiful and had the colouring of mixed heritage, maybe indigenous, black and white.

Unusually, Arlene felt a strong urge to be close to this lovely girl. By a happy coincidence, she realised Verna was a prolific reader and, at first, decided to have fun listening to the girl's mispronunciations of unfamiliar words. But Verna really was an excellent reader who read correctly and with passion. But while she laid on the lounger listening to the girl's melodious voice, the girl was plotting to move on to better herself.

When she took Verna to Kingstown with her, it was frowned on by her family and staff alike. No one understood why she made such a rash decision because her family and friends were awash with servants, and everyone speculated that it may be because she wanted Verna to administer to her personally. She enjoyed the journey on the yacht not only because she was used to sea travel but because Verna was there. The girl sat close to her mistress, trembling with fear of the sea but also with anticipation of what Kingstown had to offer. She had patted the girl's hand to reassure her a few times and was amused by her childlike awe of Kingstown when they arrived.

Her mother admonished her for bringing Verna to Kingstown; she had said there was nothing for her to do and fretted that her loyal servants would have to find something for the girl to do. So, it was decided that Verna could at least make Arlene's bed and tidy her room every day. But she rarely saw her maid for the two weeks they spent in the capital. She would spend her days chatting with her mother and her aunt Veronica and helping them with their finances. While in the capital, she would take a substantial amount of cash out of the bank for staff wages and other expenses, which was placed in a safe in her mother's bedroom.

The rest of the time she spent calling on her many family and friends, all of whom lived outside Kingstown on Dorsetshire Hill and scattered areas from Villa to Argyle on St Vincent's east or windward coast. She loved being on the main island because there was lots more to do; she didn't get bored and felt alive and purposeful. Sometimes she would think that if she didn't love Sidney as deeply as she did, she would return to her homeland in a heartbeat.

But Sidney was the perfect husband – kind, loyal, generous and hard-working. She was lucky to have such a catch and silently thanked God she wasn't lumbered with some of the sorry specimens she witnessed every day of her existence in her world.

She would do nothing to upset Sidney, who was indulgent and left her to do whatever she cared to do and go anywhere she desired. He had all his family on Bequia and never begrudged her frequent visits to her mother and to enjoy herself a little with 'her crowd'. For years, life for the couple continued on a steady and happy vein, a life far removed from the poor people of the islands, a life bathed in ease and affluence.

She had many fantasies of befriending black women but never tried to follow them up. There were well-educated middle-class women that she was acquainted with, but she never endeavoured to forge intimate friendships. Thus she was ignorant of these women's social interactions, and as time passed, she became even more emotionally distant from the black population. When she rashly took Verna to the main island, she had whetted her appetite for improvement and adventure. She became upset when the girl decided to leave Bequia to live in Kingstown, she couldn't hold her back even if she wanted to. Verna could simply have walked away. In those days, a written reference was not essential for servant work, though a word-of-mouth reference would be invaluable, especially if the would-be houseworker had proven before to be 'light-fingered'.

Arlene had visited her mother many times since Verna left Bequia, but she never bothered to find out anything about her. If she really was interested, all she had to do was ask any of her mother's servants for an update because she felt they knew something about the young woman's whereabouts.

Veronica and Beryl spent a lot of their lives sitting at the upstairs windows overlooking the main street they lived on; they were convinced they knew all about what was going on all around them in their town. The two ladies knew most of the people on sight but not personally; they also had a high-handed attitude towards their subjects, mostly the females, using scathing comments freely. They sometimes expressed their admiration of their subjects' dress and deportment, but mostly they snootily dismissed them as having no style.

Months after Verna's move to the capital, Arlene told her mother and aunt, but they were adamant the ex-maid didn't live in Kingstown because they would have recognised her walking among the throngs beneath their windows. However, they had only glimpsed her once when she stayed in their home, and of the two women, it was Veronica who took more notice of the young woman, so Arlene was unsure whether either woman would have been able to pick Verna out in a crowd. Veronica had noted Verna was tall and, as she described her to Beryl, 'handsome'. She wondered why such an attractive girl wasn't already married. With her looks, she'd be a catch, she reflected.

If only they had asked Hermie or Marlene, they would have known Verna was indeed working in Kingstown and had boarded at Hermie's for a while. But they would never have gossipy conversations with the hired help, who, in turn, would never dream of imparting gossip to their prudish employers. A 'mouthy' maid could soon find herself jobless. Verna had indeed walked right under the arches of their large, imposing house every day ever since she began working at the government office while still living at Hermie's. How they had never seen her, regardless of which side of the road she used, was surprising. Perhaps because she was not wearing a little white hat on her head and a white pinafore covering the front of her torso, clouded their perception.

Arlene sometimes joined the people watching by the window while she was engaged in conversation with her mother. She did hope she would see Verna walk past, and a couple of times she was so sure it was her that she jumped up and whispered her name. She was shocked that her heart missed a beat in anticipation. Luckily, the other ladies were too engrossed in their hobby to notice Arlene's reaction.

"Arlene, aren't you staying for Carnival next week?" Her mother asked as they settled down to supper on a visit during February, a couple of years after Verna had arrived in the capital.

"No, Mommie, I've got things to do at home. I'm helping Lucy with our celebrations at the yachting club. I've got to help this year; I was over here last year." She wanted a quieter time that year and had decided to give the low-key Bequia celebrations all her attention for a change.

"What a pity. We can see the parade from here; we don't have to leave the house at all," said her disappointed mother.

Arlene knew the drill, for it had been going on for years since she was little. Sit by the window, and you have a perfect grandstand view. How she longed to 'jump up' with the people dancing in the street, to really 'feel' the thumping of the steel band and sweat with the carefree revellers. More than once she had to be pulled back from falling out the window in her excitement. But age and elegance intervened, and now she would never dream of being down there with the sweaty masses but would carouse with her friends at their private parties instead.

She hoped to be home that Friday, so spent the few days left sorting out her affairs and making sure there was enough money in the safe to see her mother and aunt through the time before she returned again. On the Thursday before Carnival, she left the house early to go to Ratho Mill to visit a long-standing friend. She spent hours with her friend, listening to her sadness about a disintegrating marriage. She hoped her friend would find a solution quickly – divorce or learn to live with an uncaring man.

The taxi taking her back to Kingstown later that afternoon drove slowly along Back Street, the main street. Passing the library on the left side of the road, then as they were approaching the post office on the right side a little further along, Arlene let out a cry that startled the driver, and he braked suddenly. If Kingstown was awash with traffic then, in the early sixties, an accident would have been unavoidable.

"What's wrong, Miss?" The driver turned to face the alarmed lady sitting in the back.

"Nothing! Let me out here!" she demanded.

She got out of the car, handed the driver his fare, then ran towards a lady walking tall and fast away from her.

"Verna, Verna, stop, it's me, Arlene," she called out.

Verna stopped her stride abruptly and turned to face the person who called her name; she knew that voice very well. The women moved hurriedly towards each other, and before either knew what they were doing, they embraced. Verna extricated herself from Arlene's arms, looking at her ex-mistress with joyful puzzlement.

"How are you, Verna? I thought you had gone overseas!" she spoke gasping, as though out of breath.

"I've been here all the time. I..." Suddenly she was back in servant mode; she dropped her eyes and didn't know how to react to the excitement of seeing Arlene again.

"What are you doing? Where do you..." Arlene stopped; she realised she was embarrassing Verna, then she asked her to come to the house with her so that they could talk properly.

Verna sat in the rich people's downstairs living room, which she knew from being a maid there, surrounded by the two elderly residents and Arlene. A myriad of emotions swirled around inside her, but she began to soften when the ladies chatted to her as though she were an old friend. They wanted to know all about her, but Arlene banished them to another room so that she could talk to Verna alone.

She happily told Arlene her whole story from the very minute she arrived in the capital – how she couldn't find Earl, how frightened she became, and how Hermie rescued her. She described her job, her ordeal with the typing lessons, her new home, her mother, her friends and her contentment of achieving a satisfactory social level in her life. Arlene could see she was happy and found herself equally filled with joy with the young lady's progression.

"Hermie could've told mommie or auntie you were bunking up with her. It must have been quite a struggle; you could have stayed here," said Arlene.

"Oh, I forbade her telling anyone about me; I wanted to make it on my own. I got Earl out of my system pretty sharpish when no one knew who he was; he's like the 'invisible man' in the pictures. As I said, I prospered with no one's assistance well, except Hermie and her family and Mrs Walcott at work giving me a break," she said, feeling really pleased with herself.

Arlene was deeply enthralled with Verna, pleased that she had improved her life considerably, and for the first time looked on her as a true equal, smartly dressed, poised and beautifully articulate. Relaxed and complacent in the smiling girl's company, she got up and walked to a side table, picked up a small silver-coloured bell, and tingled it for the servants' attention, a signal that refreshments were required. Verna jumped up, said she had to go, and before Arlene could react, she was out of the door and dashed off.

"Verna, wait!" said a bemused Arlene.

Rage and Confusion

Verna hurried down Back Street towards River Road. Arlene stood on the sidewalk outside the front door watching the disappearing young woman but held back the urge to chase after her. She went back inside just as Hermie was placing the tray with cold drinks and small cakes on the side table. Hermie left the room without realising who the refreshments were for, but she had an inkling a female visitor had been in the room; it was filled with the sweet aroma of a perfume that reminded her of Verna. Arlene ignored the iced drinks, noiselessly scampered upstairs and with forceful anger, she slammed the bedroom door, then threw herself on her bed and wept.

Verna was shaking with rage and confusion. It was going so well at Arlene's; she had felt comfortable and relaxed in her ex-mistress' company. So, what spooked her and made her run away. It was the bell! The moment Arlene walked over to the little table and picked up the little bell, memories of having been a servant came flooding back, which filled her with shame. She had worked hard improving her station; the bell smashed that illusion.

On Carnival Tuesday, unable to get any information out of her sour daughter, Rhoda sat at one of the small windows at the front of their home, observing the merry revellers walking past on their way to play masque. She was puzzled as to why Verna was so upset when she came home in a foul mood a few days ago, refusing to discuss what was the matter. So Rhoda surmised that maybe she had lost her job or had a confrontation with a work colleague. In any case, Verna rarely left her room that weekend.

As spectators made their way to the park or to stand on the side of the town's streets to observe the celebrations, Verna and

Rhoda stayed at home. Whenever the breeze wafted the sweet sounds of the steel bands and the jubilant shouts of the revellers, Rhoda felt an urge to go and join them, but her loyalty to her sad daughter made her stay at home away from the festivities.

On Ash Wednesday morning, the day after the revelries of Carnival, Verna got up early as usual and got herself ready to go to work. She ate a piece of bread and cheese, drank her condensed milk sweetened coffee, and left the house for the office without saying much to her mother. Meanwhile, Rhoda decided to go shopping after she had attended church, where a cross of ashes was smudged on her forehead. Normally she would take the back road, passing the convent on the left side and the overgrown rear environs of the Anglican Cathedral on the other side, then pass Bishop's College, one of the town's high schools. But as she was already on Back Street, she decided to take the side street with the Methodist church on one side and the Anglican Primary School further along, nearer the seafront.

On Bay Street, she paused to admire a group of men pushing a fishing boat into the water with its flat, lazy waves calmly kissing the dark sand bordering the road. It was a good day, hot as usual with a light breeze tempering the heat of the sun already high in the sky with the approach of the middle of the day. The sky was clear of clouds and dazzlingly blue as she walked leisurely on the sidewalk, humming quietly to herself a popular Nat King Cole song, breathing in the perceived happiness all around her. She didn't get too far along when someone behind her whispered.

"Miss Rhoda!"

"Yes?" Startled, she had no idea who the lady was, but it began to dawn on her. She smiled and took the hand offered with a firm handshake.

"I thought you looked familiar, Verna's mother. I saw you briefly in Bequia."

"Ah, yes, Mrs Cassocks."

"It's Arlene; just call me Arlene. I'm visiting my mother and Aunt Veronica."

Rhoda had never spoken to Arlene before, though she had stayed in her Bequia home, but Verna had given her vivid descriptions of the Cassocks and their Kingstown relatives. When she first came to the capital, Verna showed her around, and one of the first places she pointed out was Arlene's mother's large house, which seemed to possess the highest and longest arch over the sidewalk.

They strolled towards the market, chatting about nothing in particular, but Rhoda said she was glad to be living permanently on the main island and that she loved her job at the hospital. She explained that life had changed for the better for her and Verna. Arlene in turn told Rhoda that she made regular trips over to see her mother and that a few days earlier she had bumped into Verna near the post office on Back Street.

"You spoke to Verna," said Rhoda, amazed. "She didn't say a word to me; I wonder why?"

Arlene didn't elucidate; she by-passed that but offered an invitation, "I'm returning home at the weekend, I'd like both of you to come for supper, say, six p.m. on Friday."

"Kind of you, Arlene; I'll tell Verna, and we'll confirm soon." Rhoda wasn't sure how Verna would react, seeing that she didn't mention that she had seen and spoken to Arlene.

"Lovely. See you soon." Arlene smiled and hurriedly walked off towards Back Street.

Rhoda continued until she reached and passed the noisy, bustling, chaotic market on her way to the stores. She wished it was late afternoon, then she would be able to tell Verna all about her encounter with Arlene, but she had to wait all day. She hoped the news would lift her daughter's spirits. Later that day, when she returned home from work and her mood greatly improved, Verna called out as she entered the house but didn't get an answer. Her mother was outside in the miniscule backyard tending to her equally miniscule vegetable patch.

"You're wasting your time with that lot; it's too stony round here for good yields." Verna stood practically over her mother, who was stooped low weeding and loosening the stony earth around the few plants.

"I'm determined to get something growing; it's a good spot here by the river; otherwise, those two fruit trees – the breadfruit tree and that crooked coconut tree next door – won't flourish."

"Those trees are hardy and would grow anywhere; here belongs to the river; we humans came and took it from the poor river; hence, there are so many stones around, not good for precious vegetables."

Rhoda laughed. She loved the way Verna pitied everything – the small insects that bothered them, the land crabs that destroyed the garden and ate the chickens, even the unpredictable rivers and streams. She would never dream of hurting the uninvited spiders and lizards that happily share their home but drew the line with disease-carrying, bothersome flies and mosquitoes.

"Oh, I've got news for you. Let's go inside." Rhoda didn't want Martha, the nosey next-door neighbour straining her ears to hear what was going on.

"You won't believe who I was talking to today!" She rubbed her hands in glee with the juicy news she was about to impart.

Verna kicked off her shoes and sat back in the easy chair by the window with a glass of cold ginger beer in her hand, waiting eagerly for the gossip her mother seemed to garnish most days. She leant forward, looking increasingly alarmed as Rhoda happily told her all about Arlene.

"Stop, Ma, I don't want to hear anything to do with that woman." She put her hands over her ears, trying to drown out her mother's voice.

Rhoda was shocked; she felt as though she was suddenly thrust in front of a hostile stranger. She asked for an explanation and got none. She watched open-mouthed as Verna replaced her shoes and slammed out the house. Nosey Martha must surely have heard that. Rhoda was going to ignore her daughter's tantrum but became incensed that, at her age, a young working woman shouldn't behave like a spoilt brat. She hurriedly put on her shoes and went out after her. Once outside, she looked down River Road but only saw a boy walking towards her. She looked towards the north end of River Road, where several people were coming and going. Then she thought she caught a fleeting glimpse of Verna moving fast west over the short, narrow bridge towards New Montrose, and she rushed after her.

But there was no one she knew by or close to the bridge; she stood there looking around anxiously, her heart pounding. She turned to return home but changed her mind; she walked slowly towards the Botanic Gardens close by. She sat on a low wall just inside the entrance, and for the first time since moving to the main island, a flood of home sickness washed over her; she felt very alone in her new country. She wished she was back home where her real friends were because if she had a problem, there was always someone to share and help resolve it.

"Why you crying, Miss?" It was the familiar voice of Toma, a destitute teenager who spent his days wandering around town.

Sometimes, a resident would take pity on him and give him a job sweeping up their yard or running errands.

"Ahh, Toma, it's nothing, just stuff in my eyes." She tried to sound jovial while daubing at her wet eyes.

"Ah know you cry; what the matter, Mama?" he asked sympathetically.

She decided she wouldn't lie to Toma; he may be homeless, penniless and illiterate, but he was perceptive. "I'm looking for Verna. I think she came up this way. She's upset about something."

"She's here, Mama. She up by the ponds. Ah see she sitting up there!"

Rhoda thanked Toma and asked him to come around later for some food, which he gladly accepted. Without Toma, she probably would have missed Verna in the large gardens. She rushed to her and found her just as Toma said. She lowered herself to the ground and sat next to her daughter, whose eyes were red and puffy from copious tears. She put her arms tenderly around her.

A little while passed before Verna opened up and told her mother about Arlene and the maids' call-bell. She said it cut deep, reminding her of her servant girl days, which she had tried so hard to forget. Rhoda understood and wished she could wipe her daughter's memory clean of those days. She kissed her cheek and begged her not to make such things fester within because it would only make her terminally unhappy.

However, Rhoda could see both sides; Arlene may have been insensitive and did intend to remind Verna that a low-paid office job wasn't such a big step up after all. She could have ignored the bell and called out to the maid from the door or gone to the kitchen and collected the cold drinks herself. Or maybe after a lifetime's habit, she automatically rang the bell without realising it would cause offence to an ex-maid's sensibilities. Verna seemed to her mother to be over-sensitive about her past life and wanted to erect a huge wall between her former self and her present self. Rhoda reasoned that she should not be too embarrassed about where she came from, and if people did know, she should be proud of her journey forward. Hermie and her family and her friend Lorna knew exactly where they came from, and Rhoda was sure that it was only a matter of time before others knew as well. She hoped Verna would have the backbone to resist the cruel criticisms that may come her way.

Verna became more relaxed after her mother managed to soothe her and promised that they don't ever have to curry favour with Mrs Cassocks or her kind ever again. She knew there would be challenges ahead but was sure her ambitious daughter would overcome them eventually.

Verna and her mother had just done their Saturday morning chores: washed their work clothes, cleaned the house vigorously, had their lunch, then got ready to go out. Rhoda was going up to Old Montrose to visit an elderly woman whom she had only recently nursed in hospital. Verna was going to the ice cream parlour in the town centre to meet one of her work colleagues for a chat and to indulge in a banana split.

A knock at the door interrupted their routine; neither expected anyone. Rhoda, being closest, went to the door, and standing there on the little porch looking sheepish was Arlene. She stood glued to the spot in front of Arlene, mortified that they had ignored the invitation to supper and never imagined that Arlene would ever bother with them again after such an obvious snub. Arlene stood there looking lost waiting for a reaction.

After a discomfiting pause, Verna stepped in.

"What's the problem, Mrs Cassocks?" she asked forcefully.

"Verna, how nice to see you. I was worried—"

"Nice of you to care, but we're OK. How did you know where we lived? Who told you?" Verna's voice was tinged with anger and rising.

"Don't you remember you told me you lived on River Road? I simply asked at every house until I found yours," she replied jovially. She could have added that there were less than eight houses lining the river bank, and the task of finding theirs was indeed very easy.

Rhoda intervened, "Come in, Arlene; we don't want the whole neighbourhood knowing our business."

The three women sat down in the small living room, nowhere the size of Arlene's or her mother's, but there was enough space so as not to feel claustrophobic. Rhoda offered home-made lemonade, which was eagerly accepted; even a short walk in the sun can bring on a parched throat and eager thirst. Verna sat arms folded, staring at Arlene with a mixture of curiosity and hostility; she was waiting to know why the lady was still bothering them. After a few awkward seconds of silence, Rhoda broke the ice.

"So how are you keeping, Arlene?" she asked, as though to an old friend she hadn't seen for a while.

"Good, thank you. And you?" Arlene's eyes rested on Verna even though she was talking to Rhoda.

The two women's eyes never deflected from each other, and it was Arlene who blinked first. She apologised for barging into their lives, explaining she only wanted to keep in touch, then congratulated Verna on the progression she had made since moving to the capital.

Getting no positive response from Verna, who was still

stony-faced and silent, she decided to leave. Rhoda walked her to the front door. Arlene stepped onto the narrow asphalted road, nodded and bade farewell. Feeling deflated, she began walking slowly down the road back to her mother's home.

"Wait for me!" Verna called out as she ran to catch up with Arlene just as they arrived at the crossroads connecting River Road with Victoria Park and Kingstown Park, "I'll walk you home."

"Do you mind if we take Bay Street? I feel the need for salty air," said Arlene, turning her head to see a big, warm smile filling Verna's face.

They walked in silence down to Back Street, crossed the road, and walked down the riverside, crossing Middle Street towards Bay Street and the beach. There was indeed a steady warm, salty breeze caressing their faces that made walking in the strong sun quite pleasant. As they walked slowly towards the town centre, Verna confessed that the servants' call bell had had a devastating effect on her and that her mother had helped her realise that she mustn't feel ashamed any more of where she came from.

Arlene was distraught; she had no idea that the simple act of summoning a maid would have had such a profound effect on someone who had moved forward and doing so much better for themselves. She wrongly thought Verna was tough and would not have minded if people knew she was once a maid. She apologised profusely and swore to banish the bell from her home in Bequia forever. However, she was unsure of her mother's reaction to such a drastic change of a lifelong habit at this stage of her life.

"You must think I'm a fool for reacting so badly, and I feel a little ashamed for behaving like a spoilt child. You can keep your bells; I should have acted more grown-up," she said.

"No, dear, I'm at fault here. I should've been more sensitive; you must have thought I'm a callous fool. The bells in Bequia will be no more. It has taken this incident for me to realise how demeaning we treat our house staff, like slaves of long ago. Ring the little bells; order, demand and expect obedience!"

"Oh, dear, did I start a revolution?"

"You're quite right; some of us need to be dragged into the twentieth century. I'm a modern woman and should have acted like one. I'll take you to meet my friends, and you can judge for yourself if we're all ogres enmeshed in the past."

"Won't they be offended?" Verna wasn't sure about that at all.

"I doubt it. Some are still ogres of the past, but most, at least the ones I know, are quite progressive."

Before they turned up off Bay Street towards her mother's house, Arlene did something she had never done in her life before to anyone, not even her husband. She hooked her arm around Verna's, and they walked serenely to her destination.

For the next few days before she returned to Bequia and Sidney, they became inseparable. They sat in her mother's home, sat in the River Road house, sat in the Botanic Gardens, and sat in the ice cream parlour, talking as their little ornate boats of ice cream melted into slushy liquid. They talked and talked and laughed a lot.

This being Kingstown news, soon spread fast about the two women, and it was Hermie who went around to have a chat with Rhoda. Unpleasant rumours were circulating about suggesting that Verna was the white woman's 'poodle'. Hermie thought Verna should be associating with girls her age, and perhaps it was time she had a boyfriend. Not seemingly uninterested in men was making people speculate. Rhoda was infuriated; she couldn't believe that her good friend would listen to injurious gossip about her daughter. That Hermie, whom she trusted would behave in such a matter, shocked her.

"Get away from me with your mischief; Verna is an intelligent lady and can choose whoever she wants for a friend no matter who they are; man, woman, child, black or white; you disappoint me, Hermie," she screamed. "Go away and leave us alone!"

She slammed the door in Hermie's face. Retreating indoors, she stomped through the house to stand on the river bank, behind her home. She squinted her eyes, not from wretched tears but from the stiff breeze building into a harsh wind that parched her face, ruffled her hair and whipped the big trees surrounding her into a fuming babble that matched her inner rage.

By the time Verna returned home, she had calmed down, though the elements continued to batter the house with driving rain and howling wind. She had made their supper and everything was laid out on the little table ready. They ate, not in silence but as they always did, chatting heartily and updating each other on their day's itinerary. Verna had lots to say, but her mother had little to say; she wasn't going to upset her child with spurious tittle-tattle.

Chapter 5

The Blue Letter

Their friendship sealed, Arlene returned home, and Verna and Rhoda continued happily with their lives. They became regular visitors to Arlene's family home, and though Verna felt self-conscious in the old ladies' presence, Rhoda was quite at ease and spent many happy times chatting and enjoying their company. Strangely, despite their affluent background and Rhoda's poor, semi-educated one, all the ladies seemed to be absolutely equal in their beliefs and expectations. Rhoda, however, had more knowledge of what was really going on around her and their town's environs; the old ladies appeared lonely and isolated.

Whenever Arlene came over from Bequia, she would take Verna with her to her world of rich friends, idle chat, strong cocktails, and long athletic swims on the better beaches, from Indian Bay to the slightly rougher Brighton Beach. But these outings could only occur at weekends because Verna didn't belong to Arlene's moneyed world and had to work for her living during the week. During one of those jaunts, Verna met someone she thought would be interesting to become better acquainted with. His name was Calver, and he was a barman at one of the exclusive clubs they frequented.

At first, he was no more than a polite worker wondering who the beautiful brown-skin girl was and why she was hob-knobbing with the rich whites he served. He could see she was pleasant company within that crowd but still looked like she didn't belong. He longed to find out more about her and how she came to fit in with the island's elite. But he felt it was wishful thinking on his part because a young lady from a well-healed and maybe rich family would never look his way, a mere barman. Verna would be missing from this wealthy group for weeks whenever Arlene went back home. She was not confident enough to mix with the others without Arlene, and she was soon forgotten.

Some weeks later, Calver was in town, which he rarely visited unless to buy merchandise for the club, do banking or pay bills. He preferred the country where he lived with his mother at Belmont, and if he could avoid the capital, he did. However, he hoped he could see Verna mingling with the town's crowds, then shook that improbable thought out of his mind. As the afternoon drew towards a close, the numerous schools dotted around the capital emptied, the stores and offices closing, a lot of hustling and bustling as the exodus back to suburban homes and outside the town got underway. He walked hurriedly to his battered Jeep, sharing the crowded sidewalk with many sweaty bodies when he bumped into someone. They became enmeshed in an embarrassing tangle of arms and apologies. Verna felt a kinship with the muscle-toned, nattily dressed young man. Like two children playing tag, they started giggling.

They talked and walked slowly towards his car; she said she was on her way home after doing an errand for her mother, and he said he was on his way home after doing errands for his mother and the club. They parted amicably with promises to meet again. She watched the rattling old Jeep disappear down the sparsely trafficked road, then out of sight. She stood for a while staring at nothingness, then caught herself and self-consciously hurried off.

The encounter with Calver jolted her so powerfully she found it difficult to think. At home, she waited anxiously for Rhoda to get home from work; she had a lot to tell her.

The strange feelings, which seem to make her heart pound, her throat sandpaper dry, her skin bristle with goose bumps, and an inability to think straight made her wonder if that was normal when people fell in love or was she coming down with an illness. She decided because of the confusion enveloping her that she was indeed in love. She danced around the kitchen as she cooked their supper, then Rhoda walked in out from the dark road, exhausted after a gruelling day in the hospital.

"Ma, I've wonderful news. I met a man; he's the one. I know it." She was still dancing with childish glee.

The tired Rhoda changed her work clothes, then flopped herself down on a dining chair in front of her supper, laid out ready to consume, and seemed not to hear or care. Verna continued her exaggerated tale about Calver while they ate – his stunning handsomeness, his gentle voice – she was sure that at last the right one had sashayed into her life when she wasn't even looking. Rhoda let her talk then with a straight face and the look of someone who had experienced those feelings before and had them dashed. She looked jadedly at her excited daughter.

"You sure he's not married or got heavy baggage weighing him down?" she asked.

Nothing wiped the smile off Verna's face faster than those few words. The shock realisation that she knew absolutely nothing at all about Calver except that he was a barman at one of the clubs she sometimes visited with Arlene. She became deflated and a little ashamed of her rashness. Calver dominated her thoughts every second of her waking days, though, but he was not mentioned again, at least to Rhoda. She wished Arlene would come over so that they could go clubbing again, then she could formally introduce herself to the man of her dreams.

Nevertheless, as the weeks flew by and she was still unable to get him out of her mind, she asked a work colleague who had access to a car if she wanted to visit an exclusive drinking club in the country. Selma, who shared a desk with her and had heard of her adventures with Arlene, was intrigued and agreed because she always wanted to know how the well-healed spent their leisure time.

"So how do you know of such a place?" asked Selma as they sauntered leisurely home after work. "You sure they'd let us in? I hear those places are private, for rich whites only, and we're black and poor as church mice."

"There are no segregated clubs on this land now; perhaps it was like that years ago," Verna explained. "Some people think it's still the same, but I've been with Arlene to quite a few, and I've seen well-healed people who look like us relaxing and enjoying a drink, so I know they're open to all, you just have to be able to afford their expensive drinks."

"Right, so long as you can pay for their expensive booze, they'll let you in their upper crust clubs. I get it," said Selma, not convinced about Verna's explanation.

She had heard Verna talk of Arlene many times and was amazed that women from such diverse backgrounds could be such good friends. She knew where the family lived in the town and had heard they were rich because they once owned several stores in the town. However, she decided to go with her friend that Saturday to find out why Verna was so keen to go there.

They arrived at the club, which was off the beaten track, and up a very steep hill, the place was teeming with near-inebriated people. They walked in straight and purposefully; quite a few people called out to Verna, smiling, beckoning and looking around expectantly for Arlene, but saw another lady at Verna's side instead. She acknowledged everyone with a smile and a wave but walked with Selma to the bar. They stood patiently by the bar waiting for the ice-cold cola drinks they ordered. Verna looked around for Calver. She couldn't see him and so asked the serving barman if he was on duty. He said that Calver no longer worked there and divulged that a rumour was going around that he was about to open a beach bar somewhere near Calliaqua or thereabouts, and that was all he knew.

She and Selma, glasses in hand, went over to the group of ladies crowding around a small table who had called her and wanted her to stay for a chat, but she made the excuse that she and her friend were on their way to see a friend and just popped in for a quick cold drink. After consuming their drinks, she bade goodbye, and they jumped into the car, which Selma had borrowed from a relative, and drove to the beachside area that the barman had indicated.

On the beach where they thought the bar would be, Verna was shocked to see a tiny rickety, roughly made shack of battered corrugated tin with flat stones weighing down the coconut branches on its roof. A rough wooden bench completed the scenario. The young man behind the roughly made bar counter was not Calver, but she asked him if Calver was the owner and where she could find him. The young man said he and his father owned the business, and he had never heard of anyone called Calver.

Disappointed and humiliated, she apologised to Selma for the wild goose chase she involved her in, and they returned to town. It looked like as it was with Earl a few years earlier when she first visited Kingstown; she had invented a fantasy man. She felt really stupid, especially in front of Selma, and promised herself she would never chase after a man again.

"So, it was a particular man you were looking for? Who is this elusive Calver?" Selma felt a bit used but decided to brush it aside.

"No one special, just someone I met who was kind; he's not anything to me," said a contrite Verna, who acted as though the whole exercise was done simply to show Selma a bit of Arlene's world. It was a white lie; she had hoped she may have had a chance with Calver and that he would have been the suitable man she so craved.

Rhoda had no idea where Verna had gone to but was home when Selma dropped her off. Verna went into her bedroom to escape Rhoda's curiosity about what she was up to. Lying on her bed, she eventually dozed off. Rhoda was a little concerned as to why her daughter would be taking a nap when she should be up and about; young, healthy people don't take afternoon naps.

"What's the matter, baby girl?" she called out from behind Verna's closed bedroom door. "You sick?"

Verna rolled off the bed and said she just closed her eyes because she was tired. She stretched and yawned in front of her mother to empathise with her tiredness. There were chores to do; most of the daylight had gone; she had wasted it in a fruitless pursuit and couldn't even let her mother know how silly she felt.

"They're working you too hard at the department," Rhoda observed, "you always seem harassed when you come home these days."

"We've got a lot of work to do, but we cope. It's the heat," she lied, "too hot these days."

"No more than usual, I'd say. You must be sickening for something. See a doctor, get a check-up." Rhoda began to feel uneasy about her daughter's health.

It took a lot of reassurance to put Rhoda's mind at rest because Verna didn't want her mother to see her as a sad person desperate for a man. Then the wise lady showed her daughter where her thoughts were placed.

"By the time I was your age, I had a child, so where's your husband?" she said, teasing her discontented child.

"As I said before, Ma, I'm waiting for the right man; he doesn't have to be well-off, just kind and understanding. All the ones I see around here are slackers, just wanting a good time and nothing else. I'll know when the right one comes along."

The ladies laughed, then went on enjoying the remainder of the day. A knock at the door spoilt the amity. Verna was closest, so she went to see who it was. It was Bella, one of her mother's new acquaintances from the Anglican Church they attend just down the road. Verna left the ladies to chat while she busied herself in her bedroom. After a short while, Bella left.

"Isn't that the gossipy woman who knows everybody's business?" she asked as soon as Bella exited the house.

"The same, only this time it wasn't gossip. She came to ask me to join the church committee; they're organising next year's garden party."

"You said no, of course," said Verna.

"I said I'd love to help. It's time I spread myself around a bit, and get involved. Back home, I used to help the church, but here there are so many people, they never looked in my direction. I'm happy they asked me to help." She smiled, secretly praising Verna for encouraging her to move to the main island.

After a nervous start when all she did was miss Mayron, she had at last found her niche and felt she belonged. Bella had also asked her if she would be available to help decorate the church for the flower festival in a few weeks. All this, Verna had said, sounded like people trying to abdicate their duties by passing them onto her poor, unsuspecting mother. Rhoda, however, saw this as a true welcome; she had always longed to be part of the committee organising the church activities.

Verna looked at her mother across the table as they ate supper and realised how much she had taken to the town's life and culture. She thought, a little sadly, that Mayron faded faster than she had ever imagined from their consciousness. Rhoda loved the main island and all the privileges it offered up, and for the first time in her life she had a regular wage from a job she loved, which put a little money in her purse.

Nearing the flower festival, Rhoda was the busiest she had ever been in her life. She and the committee ladies had cleaned and polished the church from top to bottom. She hardly had much time to spend with Verna, who seemed to be a little jealous of her mother's new popularity. A couple of days to go, and some flowers were to be delivered to Mrs Howard's in Middle Street, where the ladies would sort and build displays before transporting them to the church for the two-day festival at the weekend. A harassed Bella hurried over the Wednesday before the festival, to beg Rhoda to accept some of the flowers which would be coming from a lady in the country. Mrs Howard had taken ill and was in the hospital, and Bella said it was not convenient for her to take them and couldn't find anyone else to take the flowers in their home.

Rhoda, of course, said she would love to help and that there was ample space for the flowers in her house. Verna was horrified and argued with her mother over that decision; she felt she should have been consulted first. She wanted to point out that it was her name on the rental agreement but pulled back, not wanting tension with her mother, who paid her share equally. She sulked thereafter and avoided her mother as much as she could in the small house. She decided that when the flowers were delivered, she would make herself scarce till supper time. Thankfully, she thought, they would be all gone by Friday to their final destination in the church.

She was right; the house was full of people and flowers when she got home from work, and her mother was truly in her element, enjoying every second of it. She tip-toed and side-stepped around to her room, then waved as she left the house. Rhoda was too engrossed to notice her disapproving daughter. When she arrived back home, it was almost dark, and all the ladies had gone. However, the house was still taken over with perfumed aromas and beautiful displays of flowers ready for transportation, many lying expectantly in buckets of water, indoors and outside in the yard.

"Don't worry, darling, they'll be all gone tomorrow. The church will look splendid by the time we're finished. Oh, such a lovely smell." Rhoda was proud of her part in the creations.

"I hope I can sleep; the smell's overpowering; too many flowers in this little room," said Verna.

"It's just for one night; you'll survive," replied Rhoda.

Verna couldn't wait for morning so she could get out of the florist shop her home had become. Though it was temporary, she felt a sort of permanency pervading because her mother seemed completely hooked and she could see their home being used for all sorts of things to do with the church thereafter. When she left work late Friday afternoon, she hoped her mother and her friends would have cleaned up their mess so she could just concentrate on relaxing and whining down from a busy day at the office. She was lucky; the house was empty of its fragrant loads and already cleaned up.

She kicked off her shoes and went barefoot out to the kitchen to see if her mother had started supper. There were tri-tri cakes fried and ready to eat; she helped herself to a few, poured a large glass of Mauby, turned the radio on to the mellow tone of Nancy Wilson filling the house, and returned to the easy chair she usually sat on to relax. The tri-tri was gone, the glass nearly empty when she was disturbed by loud, urgent knocking at the front door, which nearly made her jump out of her skin. Seeing Bella at the door angered her, but she greeted her politely.

"Hello Verna, your mother sent me for the big stool. She say it's in the kitchen," said Bella timidly.

"OK," said Verna, careful not to show annoyance because if she did, Bella would spread it to all and sundry that she was rude, and it would backfire on Rhoda. She went to fetch the stool while Bella waited by the front door.

"Ah wonder, Verna," she said as Verna handed over the stool, "if you can bring it to church for me. It's my back, bad today!" She rubbed her backside to empathise with where the pain was and was pleasantly surprised that Verna was happy to take the stool to the church for her.

When Bella left, Verna cursed under her breath but immediately admonished herself for being mean to her mother, who was trying to make their lives pleasurable and worthwhile. She put her shoes back on, picked the tall stool up, and walked down the road the short distance to the church. Rhoda was pleased to receive the stool and took it away to adorn as a display. Verna was impressed; the church looked magnificent; she had never seen anything like it before; there was never such adornment in their plain little church on Mayron.

The dedication service that Saturday afternoon was packed

with regular and irregular churchgoers alike who came to admire or gawk at the church committee's artistic floral exhibition. Verna was really proud of her mother and said a prayer of thanks for having such a good person for her mother. There was so little to do on Mayron that it was easy to sit around all day feeling sorry for yourself and concentrating on every little ache and pain.

Rhoda did help out in the church, cleaned it and the little school, in addition to the laundry service she undertook for the tiny, affluent few, especially Mrs Lamour. But she was diminishing from lack of stimulation. Her move to the main island was the making of her, and she was so busy that Verna hardly saw her some days. When she first came over, she stayed close to the lodgings at Mrs Darrow's and felt afraid and out of her depth. But slowly, with her new friend Hermie's help, she acquainted herself with the town and made herself friendly, popular and available.

Verna was different, though a little aloof, she craved for friends, popularity and most of all, a suitable man. Unfortunately, she rarely tried to forge friendships, and though she was friendly with all of her work colleagues, the only one she could call a close friend was Selma. She rarely saw her Bequia friend Lorna, who was married with a family and still worked full time at the hospital, which gave her little time to socialise. However, a major event would occur that would test Verna's resolve.

A Mission from Abroad

A blue letter from England with Queen Elizabeth the Second's head emblazoned on the integrated stamp was delivered to their home. The address was beautifully written with the careful tenderness of a calligrapher; she stared at her name and address with childlike awe.

"Well, have you never seen a letter before?" asked her mother, who was keen to know who sent a letter for her daughter all the way from England, and why?

Verna walked slowly to a chair and sat down; her mother hovered close by. It could have been from her friend Muriel from Bequia, Sadie, a new friend from her boarding days, or Angel, another new friend and ex-colleague, all of whom had moved permanently to England. She carefully turned it over, savouring the moment of delight of the familiar name to be revealed. It was a complete shock seeing Arlene's name where she never expected it to be. They had only heard a few days previous, when Rhoda visited Mrs Lorraine and her sister, that Arlene was abroad, and they assumed she had gone to Barbados, a regular haunt. It shook them up that she had gone so far away without so much as a word, not even to her so-called best friend Verna.

"Well, that's a surprise; her mother said she was overseas, so I thought she was in Barbados," said Rhoda.

"It would have been polite to let us know she was going to England," said Verna with anger building, "that's so disrespectful. With a friend like that, who needs enemies?"

She tore the letter open angrily, even ripping through some of the words. Rhoda, feeling disgusted with Arlene's behaviour, walked away to the backyard while Verna read the letter. She read it twice, then went into her bedroom, closed the door behind her, and read it again. Arlene wrote that she wasn't sure when she and Sidney would return, and her words were full of contrition for abandoning Verna and not getting in touch sooner. She said their move to England was sudden and unplanned, but they would return as soon as Sidney was ready.

She got the impression that Arlene had had enough of England and wanted to return home. They were already away for over a month, but Arlene's loyalty to her husband meant she would continue to support him in whatever he chose to do. Then there was a request that threw Verna into a tizzy; Arlene wanted her to go to Bequia.

She called her mother to come in from the backyard and thrust the letter into her hand. "I can't believe it; look what she wants me to do. Incredible!"

Rhoda held the blue letter a little off in front of her and began to read. The first half of the letter was full of warmth and friendliness, but the rest, though not quite obvious, had the tone of an indirect order.

"Well, I never; I can't make this woman out. Is she a friend or feigning friendship? How dare she?" The ordinarily unruffled Rhoda felt rage building within.

The letter became the focus of conversation for the ladies; they were unable to make up their minds what to do. Each would agree to ignore it, then change their minds, wanting to follow the instructions contained exactly. The decision was made for them when Hermie, back on speaking terms with Rhoda, came with a message from Mrs Lorraine who wanted to see them both as soon as possible. Verna didn't want to go, but Rhoda thought with the advent of the letter they should go to see what the problem was and why they were involved.

Beryl greeted them as though she hadn't seen either for ages. There was quite a bit of small talk which began to irritate Verna before Rhoda asked why she wanted to see them both urgently.

"Sorry, Arlene didn't get in touch before; she asked me to have a chat with you about Bequia. Would you be able to help her?" Beryl sounded a little too friendly for Verna's liking.

"Verna got a letter all right, but she won't be doing as she asked. Why can't Arlene get one of her husband's people or friends to do what she wants? It's wrong to involve us," said Rhoda with more than a hint of irritation in her voice.

"She could have asked any number of people known to her in Bequia or over here, but she told me she prefers someone she trusts and who would be sympathetic," said Beryl.

"So," retorted Verna, "she trusts us more than family to throw people away, kick them out of their jobs, with no money forthcoming, and become even more destitute than they already are. Sorry, we won't be doing that!"

"Arlene's a good person; she really doesn't like upsetting people, and she thought you may be better at explaining things to them than people they don't know," replied Beryl.

"The staff didn't ask to be left in limbo, not knowing if they have jobs or not. Oh, just ask the ex-maid to do the dirty deed; sack them all; they'll surely remember that!" said Verna, spitting with anger.

"No, not sack anyone; just lay them off until she returns. She doesn't know when they'd come back, and she knows the situation for these poor people. She did give them a couple of weeks extra pay, but now she doesn't know when she'd be back and thought they could look elsewhere for work if they can," Beryl reasoned.

"OK, I'd go and deliver the bad news to the unsuspecting staff and lock the house up properly as she wants, but I don't know when I'd be able to go over," Verna spoke with such confidence that Beryl was a little thrown.

"I'd reimburse you for the travel and expenses. Stay in the house while you're over there," said Beryl, a little happier that the ladies were going to help her daughter.

As they walked back home cogitating about the mission, Rhoda said, "I don't think you should've agreed to help; Arlene shouldn't have abdicated her responsibilities to others, the gall of the woman." Rhoda found the whole affair puzzling and was amazed that Verna agreed to face her former colleagues again. She decided that whatever she decided, she would accompany her to Bequia.

Verna intended to go to Arlene's over the weekend but was relieved when her manager offered her an extra day off in lieu. She accepted, and mother and daughter set sail on the early morning ferry the following Friday. They stepped down from the jetty into a launch, and as it pointed out towards the Grenadines, they and everyone else strained their necks to look at the building work going on at the new deep-water harbour installation. There were huge cranes sticking out of the water, large flat barges filled with aggregate, and plenty of workmen already sweating away at the new construction that early in the morning.

"End of an era when that is done," said an elderly man sadly, "this jetty done for. Next thing, demolish—"

"Nah," interrupted a young sailor, "that one for big ships, cruise liners and things like that. This jetty for pleasure tours with boats like this one."

He looked really pleased with himself for suggesting what the jetty could be used for in the future; some passengers nodded in agreement. The old man was not impressed; he sucked his teeth in disgust. Verna didn't care one way or the other, which jetty she embarked from; she just wanted the journey over and done with as soon as possible. She loved the sea to swim and frolic in but hated its unpredictability and the grief it sometimes brought to these small islands. The sea was flat calm, and there was no stiff breeze, but that didn't matter because the launch, being an oversized motor boat, ran on an engine and not sails. It was a new addition to the ferry service to the Grenadines but not owned by the Cassocks; however, Verna thought it was overcrowded and too low in the water.

It moved swiftly and smoothly through the flat water; nevertheless, the ladies were relieved when their feet touched the ground on beautiful Bequia less than an hour later. They walked along the narrow coast road then inland before reaching a pathway upwards towards the large, imposing house dominating the hillside facing Port Elizabeth. Rhoda panted as they ascended.

"I haven't climbed a hill in ages; my legs don't like this at all," she said, pausing for a breather.

"It's not that bad, Ma; this is a small hill, not a mountain. Look, we're here." She pointed to the house looming in front of them.

They sat on a couple of chairs on the veranda, which seemed to have been put out especially for them. The loungers, tables and other furniture that Verna knew so well were missing; it brought back bittersweet memories of her being a maid. After recovering from the climb, Rhoda opened the basket she was carrying and shared fried fishcakes and fried bakes with Verna, then she poured some lukewarm, sweetened milky coffee from a small flask into an enamel cup for herself. Verna poured herself some ice-cold Mauby from a larger flask into a hardened plastic glass she dug out from the basket. They ate in silence then began to question why they came over at all.

"Well, I suppose we better go back down the town and ask around for somewhere to stay, then go back home. It was folly coming here; you shouldn't have accepted Arlene's problems," said Rhoda.

"OK, let's go!" Verna jumped up, picked up her grip, and before Rhoda could react, she was half-way down the path.

"Ladies, ladies!" called a male voice coming from behind them from the side of the house.

They turned to see the very man who had given Verna a job some years before. He hobbled to them and apologised for being late.

"Mr Vernon, nice seeing you again" – Verna rushed to him – "you're limping. What's the matter?"

"Nothing bad, just pains from a lifetime of kneeling on damp earth, I guess. Anyway, where you are going? The house ready for you, come!" He turned and walked haltingly towards the house, indicating that the ladies should follow him.

He explained that Mrs Dawn, Mrs Cassocks' sister-in-law, told him all about them coming and said he must assist them in every way. Verna said she was puzzled as to why Arlene's friends or family couldn't do what she wanted.

"Ah guess coming from you would be more sensitive instead of some rich lady," Vernon tried to explain.

"I see, but what about you? Couldn't you do it?" asked Verna.

"Mrs Cassocks gave us all some pay for a couple of weeks when she left, but it's over a month now. I guess she worry about us and thinks it best to lay us all off if she don't know when she coming back. I can survive, but Bernice and the others will starve with no money coming in," he explained sadly.

Verna wished she had taken the money offered by Beryl so she could help the poor staff. She felt like a fool for not planning her mission properly and was filled with sadness for her former co-workers. The ladies never expected to have the run of the Cassock's home; each thought they would be ensconced in the servants' quarters; having the run of the house made them nervous. Vernon left them to settle in and said he'd be back later.

"Well, with all this, she wants to sack people!" Rhoda's anger was unabated, and she showed her discontentment with the situation they found themselves in.

"I feel for the staff; after all, I know these people," said Verna sadly.

Rhoda, feeling a little too uncomfortable in the house, spent most of the time seated on the veranda. Looking out over Port Elizabeth tempered her mood; she had forgotten how beautiful the tiny islands of the Grenadines were, and she began to feel homesick.

When Vernon returned, she expressed her reluctance to get further involved in the domestic intricacies of the Cassocks family. She said she would wander around the town instead, but Verna begged her to stay and support her. So the three of them walked away from the house along a narrow pathway upwards onto the ridge, then continued walking eastwards towards the Atlantic Ocean. Vernon hobbled ahead of the ladies, and despite his troublesome knees, he was leaving them behind.

Not long afterwards, just as Rhoda began complaining again, they arrived in front of a very small house resting precariously on thick crooked wooden stilts. The sad-looking house was in need of serious repair and clearly hadn't seen a pot of paint for decades. The old rotting planks, filled with holes stuffed with paper, were blackened by the relentless starkness of the tropical sun. Verna felt herself trembling as Vernon called out and the half-broken door opened to reveal a frail old lady almost bent double. Verna and Rhoda held back while Vernon hobbled to the door, giggling like a mischievous child. The lady at the door looked confused.

"What you want, eh, what you say? Speak up, man!" ordered the impatient senior.

"Marnin! Ah say, how are you doing, Miss Hilda?" Vernon shouted.

The old lady squinted and rubbed her eyes before recognition came to her. She knew Vernon since he was young, but as the years passed and she grew old and infirm she saw less and less acquaintances while she lingered on her hilltop home. Vernon explained his mission, then introduced her to the two women behind him. She said Bernice wasn't at home but can be found tending to their food plot further along the trail path. Then she retreated into the house, closing the porous door behind her.

"You don't expect us to go further along this God-forsaken mountain, do you, Mr Vernon?" Rhoda said sarcastically.

"Maybe we come back tomorrow," he replied.

"You two go back. I'll hang around and wait for Bernice to return," Verna's voice told her mother not to object. "See you soon!"

"OK. You sure now?" asked Rhoda.

"Yes, yes. I'll see you later."

The others returned to the Cassocks' home while Verna wandered around the cluttered, untidy yard in front of the rotting old house. She eventually found a tree trunk to sit on and began to form the words and the tone in which to say them when Bernice returned. She was lost in thought when she heard a familiar voice.

"My goodness, that you, Verna!" cried Bernice.

She turned to see a bedraggled, well-aged Bernice dragging herself towards her. She rushed to her; she wanted to cry at the sorry sight of such a proud, decent person descended to such poverty. They sat down on the tree trunk; hugs, tears and reminiscences followed, then the old lady reappeared at the door.

"You back, B, why did you stay so long? I was worrying!" said her housemate Miss Hilda, concerned and irritated in equal share. She made a sucking sound with her toothless mouth, then gingerly sat herself down on the top step where she had stood before.

"All right, Hilda, stop worrying," said Bernice, wiping her face, clearing her throat and regaining her dignity. "Poor thing, she worries about me all the time."

"Is she your relative, Miss B?" Verna wanted to ask lots of questions about the situation Bernice was in but refrained from embarrassing the dear lady any further.

"No, but I know her from way back, years!"

Bernice then related why she was living with Hilda. She had intended to move into a little house near Hope Bay with her Baptist church's help after the Cassocks left for England, but circumstances prevented it. She came up the hill to see Hilda before moving to Hope Bay and the church's patronage, but her friend was sick, so she stayed to help her and found it difficult to leave the frail old lady alone now. She tried to encourage Hilda to move with her, but the old girl is just too weak to walk so far, and Bernice is trapped there with no external help.

Verna was reeling with sadness and couldn't tell Bernice the true reason she came to Bequia. She couldn't understand why Arlene didn't let Bernice continue living in their house while they were away; after all, she had a room not connected to the main part of the house and had lived there since the days of Mr Cassocks' parents. Anyway, she lied about coming over to see some of the old staff she once worked with; Bernice appeared to believe her and hugged her tightly.

"Ah hear you got a top job in the government; ah proud of

you," said Bernice.

Verna corrected her about her 'top job' then proceeded to fill her in about her new life on the main island. She apologised for not keeping in touch, and she promised she would make things right for her with or without Mrs Cassocks help or approval. Bernice looked at the beautiful creature in front of her and was glad it turned out well for the ambitious girl; she thanked her for caring and told her never to change.

Before she left the old ladies, Verna opened her purse, which contained a hard earned fifty dollars, and pressed twenty dollars in Bernice's hand. Though she protested, she accepted the money, she knew refusing it would be folly when she was near starving.

Verna cried all the way back to the Cassocks' house and decided there and then that Arlene was no friend; how could she treat people like expendables? Her anger drove her along the path and back to the house at record speed. She rushed past Rhoda and Vernon, who were sitting and chatting on the veranda, grabbed her things and ordered her mother to follow her. They were not going to stay another second in the Cassocks' home, she insisted.

She stood on the pathway in front of the house waiting for her mother, who had grabbed her things without questioning why the change of heart. Vernon looked shocked; he scratched his head, did a full 360-degree turn but couldn't find the words to ask what was going on. He watched the ladies walk away from the house, then went back and locked up the house before hobbling home to his wife. It's strange, thought Rhoda, that the 'home' Verna was referring to was on the main island and not Mayron.

They went to a house Verna knew took in short-term stop-overs when main island people came to Bequia for a visit. They were lucky and got a room to share; they paid up for the night, then decided to have a wander around Port Elizabeth. Verna wanted to know if Elisha had found other work in Bequia or did she return to her impoverished family in Canouan; she hoped the resourceful lady would have found something to do somewhere. Port Elizabeth is tiny, and if she thought she could wander around without anyone recognising her, it was naivety in the extreme. It wasn't long before someone called her name.

"Verna, you come back!" called out a lady standing in front of a large, wooden tray stuffed with roasted peanuts, small flat sugary coconut cakes and slender tart ginger sticks.

Verna squinted in the bright sun shine, shielding her eyes with her hand, trying to focus; she didn't recognise the voice.

"It's me, Joycelyn; Lorna is my sister; she's nursing over in Kingstown." She rushed forward to hug Verna.

"Yes, I remember you. How are you doing, Joycelyn?" She barely remembered Lorna's older sister but was grateful for a friendly face.

Verna introduced her mother, explaining to Joycelyn they were visiting but returning to Kingstown the next day. Joycelyn, whose life had not changed an iota for years and who hardly sold anything that day, was grateful when Rhoda all but cleared her tray, filling her bag with the sugary 'sweets' which she would mostly scoff herself.

"Thank you, Rhoda, God bless you! Ah hear the Cassocks gone bust; they had rooms full of money, but rumour says that they ran to England to escape money lenders." Joycelyn licked her lips as she told the rumoured tale.

Verna laughed, but Rhoda admonished Joycelyn for believing such a baseless rumour and put her straight that the Cassocks were on holiday. She told Joycelyn as though telling off a naughty child that if the couple had suddenly gone penniless, how could they finance themselves in rich, expensive England for so long? Besides, they had lots of rich relatives both on Bequia and the main island who could support them in every way. Joycelyn rubbed her chin in concentration; it made sense what Rhoda said. She felt a little silly spreading baseless rumours.

"But everybody say so!" she insisted.

"Nobody outside their family knows why the Cassocks are away and when they'd be back, so I suggest we don't speculate or spread rumours," replied Verna calmly.

"Well, what about the servants? All scattered, left with no money. Is that how you treat good, loyal people?" asked Joycelyn, determined to get in the last word.

With those angry words ringing in their ears, they walked hurriedly away towards the eastern edge of Port Elizabeth, where the road petered out with a small cafe blocking the way. They sat down at one of the two small tables outside under a galvanised canopy to shield the searing sun off their heads. They ordered cola drinks, which were served in tall glasses filled with ice. They sat quietly sipping the cold drinks, mulling over Joycelyn's words.

"Something's bad going on; Arlene's not straight with us. I don't like it!" Anger was rising faster in Verna than she cared; her index finger on her right hand tapped the little table in front of them with a rapid urgency.

"Looks like all and sundry know about the Cassocks and we know nothing." Rhoda's mind was in a whirl.

She didn't want to ask any local person if they knew what was going on, but she wanted to hear the full, accurate story from someone. She touched Verna to stop her tapping and continued thinking. With their drinks almost consumed, she got up and walked over to the lady who had sold them the drinks and asked her a few questions. They talked for a while before the lady pointed east towards thick tropical woodland, Rhoda thanked the helpful lady, beckoned to Verna and they walked slowly out of Port Elizabeth.

"Where are we going? This is the jungle, and we didn't bring a cutlass," Verna said but obediently followed, finding it a tedious exercise in the hot sun.

"We're going to see Arlene's cousin. Perhaps she can shed some light on the situation; I feel we're not getting the full truth about what's the real reason she needed you. Then, we will go home tomorrow."

They followed a well-worn pathway through the jungle, which eventually ended close to a beach. They arrived drenched with sweat and puffing at a boatyard at least a mile away. Verna hoped she didn't smell of spent perspiration, and Rhoda hoped they got the answers to Arlene's enigmatic trip to England. When they arrived at the beach, they could see Mustique isle right in front of them. Rhoda's heart skipped a beat because behind that little island, but much further down in the southern sea, past other tiny islands and islets, lay her forsaken home, Mayron.

Carl and Priscilla

The boatyard, which was a large area partly sheltered with a flat galvanised roof, was full of boats of varying sizes in various stages of build and repair but was devoid of human workers. Just as they thought the place was abandoned, a tanned, burly man with unruly blond hair, a dirty vest top, and well-worn shorts approached the women.

"Hello, ladies, can I help you?" he asked, smoothing his hair back and wiping the sweat off his forehead.

"Afternoon, sir, we're looking for Mr Cassocks. Are you him?" asked Rhoda politely.

"Yes, that's me; the name's Carl. How can I help you?" A smile lit up his face, which relaxed the ladies.

Rhoda explained they were visiting, and they just wanted to know when Arlene and Sidney were coming back to Bequia from their British sojourn. Carl led the ladies into his tiny office, offered them rum, which they declined, poured one for himself, and chatted amiably about everything except his cousin and his wife. After a while and realising they were not going to get any information from Carl, the ladies excused themselves and started to leave. Carl stopped them and asked them to come to his home later that afternoon to meet his wife, Priscilla, whom he said would be better at filling them in.

"No one tells me anything, and I don't want to know either," he said sheepishly. "Anyway, I live there." He pointed to a not-so-grand single-storey wooden house laid back and partly hidden in the vegetation a little way from the boatyard. "See you later, around five, OK?"

"OK, five," said Rhoda.

Walking back through the jungle towards Port Elizabeth, Verna said with an air of resignation, "Are you mad, Ma? We don't know these people. I feel uneasy around here; it's too remote and too quiet for my liking. We shouldn't come back."

"Don't be silly; this is Bequia, not some large, crowded city full of murderous people. Haven't you ever heard of Carl or his wife from Arlene? Surely she must have said something about her relatives over here."

"Never a word, and I never thought to ask either. Come to think of it, neither Elisha nor Bernice ever said a thing about the Cassocks' relatives," replied Verna.

"This is a small place; everyone should know their neighbours, but I guess the rich are a different kettle of fish."

"Yea, they never tell the likes of us anything about themselves. I'm not sure we should go, Ma; after all we don't know these people; he looks like a drunk and a bit too friendly." Verna was finding her first visit back to Bequia too complicated to handle.

"We should go if we want answers, and if we feel too uncomfortable with them, we'll walk away. Does that meet with your approval?"

"OK. But we should let somebody know where we're going."

"I'll let the lady at the guesthouse know; she can send in the police if we don't return by morning."

Verna nodded rapidly in agreement, then realised her mother was making fun of her; she gave a little ironic laugh. They soon returned to the town but had to do it all over again in a few hours, to Verna's displeasure. Carl's wife Priscilla greeted the ladies profusely; she was about Arlene's age and turned out to be chatty and friendly but clearly lonely. She offered the ladies rum cocktails, which they declined, but they gladly accepted the high glasses of iced soft drinks instead. They all sat in the wide gallery, and through the trees on one side, they could see the sea looking choppy and restless, with white crests bobbing up and down as though in a crazy West Indian dance. On the other side, the boatyard loomed large, spoiling the tropical panoramic view.

Rhoda tried repeatedly to bring the conversation to Arlene; Priscilla, however, was evasive. She preferred to talk about the nuances and different tastes of the many different rums, gins and cocktails crammed on a little table in front of them. The trees stood silent and ghostly on an eerily windless evening, in front of the sinking sun already deep down into the quiet waters of the Caribbean Sea, its top rim's light dimming fast. Verna could see the sinking sun and was worried about walking back through the darkened 'jungle' and deserted Port Elizabeth back to the Bed and Breakfast.

She said, "We've got to get back now; we've an early start back to St Vincent tomorrow."

"Stay for supper; don't worry about the dark; we'll get you back safely to your hotel; we got large, bright flashlights." Priscilla was doing all she could to keep them a little longer in her company.

"We're all right, thank you; we have already arranged supper," Rhoda lied; all they had was the few left-over bits from lunchtime, which wasn't much.

"Please," said Priscilla, pleading, "we have more than enough to share. Come, it's ready!"

They followed her into the much smaller house than Arlene's, towards a four-seater dining table further into the room and close to a tiny kitchen. The table was laid with fried breadfruit, saltfish, fried plantains, salad arranged on a large platter, and a few small bread rolls. They sat down, and the merry Priscilla ordered the ladies to eat up, but the 'drunks' hardly touched a thing.

"So, when's Arlene coming home?" asked Verna over the loudness of the jolly couple.

"Coming home?" screamed Carl between loud, raucous laughter. "Never, I think they are gone for good!"

"Don't listen to him; he lies! They're coming back, one

day!" Giggled his wife.

After they finished eating, the ladies realised that they weren't getting anywhere with the inebriated pair, so they got up to leave. The couple begged them to stay longer, but Rhoda pointed out it was nearly eight o'clock and they had to get up early for the morning ferry. This seemed to focus Priscilla, who clearly didn't want to see the only people to visit her home for a while, leave. She walked, a little unsteadily, with the ladies outside through the gallery and down the few steps from the house. She asked them again how long they were staying in Bequia. Verna repeated again that they were leaving the next morning and thanked Priscilla for entertaining them so beautifully. She saw tears flowing from Priscilla's tanned, round face.

"What's the matter?" she asked.

"Nothing much; just hate seeing people leave. I like company," she replied, sobering up a bit.

"Well, at least you have your husband; some people don't even have that," said Rhoda.

"He's useless! I hardly see him, just sleep, eat and nothing else. I wish I was on the main island; at least there's more happening over there. It's too quiet for me here now. As I grow older, I get more and more lonely every day," she said passionately. The ladies stopped to comfort Priscilla, and soon the three of them were sitting on the wooden steps chatting. Rhoda always thought women like Priscilla were privileged, confident and content; sitting next to her, she saw a lonely, friendless person.

She said, "Perhaps if Arlene was here, you two could keep each other company."

"She never bothered with me; I think she and her friends

think I'm too thick for them. I never went to high school, and they look down on me." Tears were flowing freely, but her voice started to sound defiant.

"But all you rich people have higher education—" started Verna.

"Nooo," Priscilla interrupted, "not all of us are rich or got higher learning. Arlene's the well-educated and rich lady; moneyed family and married money – we're nothing like her. See how we live; does this say rich? Carl is his cousin's employee; our families are the poor lot." She paused to catch her breath, and silence ensued. Verna was shocked; she had spent so much time naively fantasising that all white people in the islands were awash in money. She never dreamt some of them would be struggling hand-to-mouth like so many black people were.

Rhoda, however, was unimpressed, "Lady, you have shelter, your husband got a job, and you have food on the table; that's a lot more than many people in all these islands have. Stop feeling sorry for yourself and change your life if you don't like it, or shut up and live it."

This really sobered Priscilla up; she apologised, then divulged all she knew about Arlene. The couple were in England, not on an elongated holiday but working in a large London hotel owned by another cousin who had done well in England. They weren't staff, but though there was a manager, they were temporarily overseeing the hotel for their relative, who was very ill and who didn't trust strangers to run his business while he was incapacitated; hence, the cousins were asked to fulfil that role temporarily.

The couple thought they would be doing it for a few weeks, but the sick cousin was taking longer to recover. They had hoped to return home quickly and felt upset for abandoning their staff, leaving them unemployed and suffering.

"But she wanted me to lay people off!" Verna shouted.

"No, not sack them, but to give them the opportunity to find something else to do if possible to earn. Arlene doesn't want them to suffer," reasoned Priscilla.

"But they are suffering; she abandoned them! Bernice has nowhere to live after living for most of her life in that big house; she's shacking up with a destitute old woman in a tiny, rotting old house. Poor Vernon is struggling without money and a sick wife, and God knows how Elisha, her young children and all the others are coping in Canouan," said Verna, her voice strident with emotion.

"I didn't think of that, I feel bad now. Tomorrow I'll talk to my cousin, Rose; she's richer than all the family put together, and see if she can help them. Arlene can pay her back when she returns," Priscilla seemed to have genuinely sobered up.

"So why didn't she ask you or your cousin Rose to do her dirty work in the first place? Why ask Verna? She's not family," said Rhoda, irritated by the whole saga.

"I guess she trusts you and thinks you can handle the situation better than any of us. She likes you, Verna; she told me so." Priscilla seemed more relaxed.

There was a moment of silence as the ladies pondered. Verna and Rhoda were thinking of what to do next, and Priscilla was mooching over her continuing loneliness, racking her brains on how to keep the ladies longer in her company.

Verna was the first to react, "Thanks for supper, Priscilla, we better get going!"

Before Priscilla could react, Verna sped off, with her mother running after her in the darkened forest. Back at the guesthouse, the two ladies remained silent, unable to make sense of the past day's offering; eventually they went to bed and slept fitfully.

It was early morning, the day already bright with the sharp, tropical sun, a few wispy clouds drifting slowly over Port Elizabeth, and the heat was building. Verna and her mother walked the short distance from the guesthouse to the little jetty to board the launch, when Priscilla approached them.

"Morning friends," she said cheerfully. "I'm coming with you; I'm going to have a life. I'm done here."

What could the others say? It wasn't their business what this fortysomething lady did with her life, so they didn't comment or ask questions until the boat set off.

"Your husband OK with you leaving?" asked Rhoda.

"Don't know; don't care! He's still in a drunken stupor. For once I'm going to live!" She sat on her two grips and clutched her handbag close to her belly, smiling the self-satisfied smile of a deed well done.

Feeling uneasy that nothing would be done for her poor friends, Verna asked, "Did you speak to your cousin Rose about Arlene's staff?"

"Yep, she knows now, and she said she'd track them done and pay them all off and put Bernice in better accommodation; she knew her from way back. I rang her first thing, early; in fact, I woke her up." She tittered as she remembered with relish the confusion she caused her cousin.

Thank God! I hope the staff will be taken care of properly now, thought Rhoda.

As the launch neared its destination, Verna and Rhoda felt increasingly anxious while Priscilla was brimming with joy. She had not been to the main island for quite a while but often wished she lived there permanently.

"Where are you going to stay?" asked Rhoda, worried that

Priscilla would want to live with them.

"Don't worry about me, ladies; I've lots of family and friends over here; it's all taken care of. Thanks for your company. See you around!" And with that, she spritely jumped off the launch onto the jetty and rushed off, laden with her wares.

"What on earth was that all about? Imagine leaving her husband just like that," said Rhoda.

"Not our business, Ma; she seems a bit cracked. I don't want to associate with that lot any more; they definitely are not our kind of people," replied Verna.

"I agree." And they walked leisurely through the town centre to their home on River Road.

Chapter 6

A Suitable Man for Verna

It took the ladies weeks to recover from their Bequia excursion, and just as they were getting back into their usual everyday lives, they were once again thrust into someone else's misadventure. They were roused in the middle of the night by urgent knocking on their front door. They slowly and silently crept, hearts pounding, to the front door, listening for signs for who was at their door at that ungodly hour. When the knocking persisted and, hearing loud sniffing sounds as though someone was crying, Rhoda called out strong and masterfully, asking who was there and what they wanted; the answer stunned her.

"It's me, Priscilla. Please, can I come in? I've nowhere to go!"

Verna opened a window a fraction and peeped to see if it was indeed Priscilla and if she was on her own. She nodded to her mother, who opened the door to a drunken, dishevelled woman who stumbled into the house and staggered to the nearest easy chair.

"What happened? Why aren't you with your family?" Verna asked, irritated that they were lumbered with an unwanted problem.

Rhoda, seeing Priscilla's distress, fetched a small towel, which she dampened before handing it to her. Priscilla wiped her face, neck and arms, then put the cloth on her face and wept into it. The others sat in front of her patiently waiting for answers, but none came.

"OK, I'm off to bed; I've to get up early for work." Verna walked off to her bed. She glanced at her bedside alarm clock while settling back on her pink sheet on her comfortable double mattress; it was nearly half past midnight. She was sleepy, but sleep was slow in coming after it was interrupted so abruptly.

"Luckily. I'm off tomorrow, so we can talk if you want to, Priscilla," said Rhoda.

"I hate that old witch. When she thought it was a temporary stay-over, she welcomed me, but once I said I'm not going back to Carl, the bitch threw me out. Can I stay here just for tonight? Tomorrow I'll go to my family up the 'hill'. They won't judge me like you know who."

"We don't have a spare bed, but you can have mine; I'll squeeze in with Verna. The WC and shower are through that door," she said, pointing to a back door. She looked at the sobbing Priscilla and felt a rush of pity for the desolate creature in front of her.

"Thank you, Rhoda; I'm grateful."

Verna had left for work, and it was another hour before Priscilla roused from her post inebriated slumber. She tidied up, ate the breakfast prepared by Rhoda, then gathered up her bags, ready to leave.

"Sorry about last night. I'll never forget your kindness, and your bed was quite comfortable; I slept well, like a log."

They walked to the front door, and Rhoda reassured Priscilla that they were there if she ever needed them again. Priscilla smiled and, laden with her bags, which she called all her worldly goods, she hurried off down River Road. Rhoda spent a great deal of time that day trying to get Priscilla out of her head, a woman she didn't really know but who she could see was lonely and vulnerable.

While eating supper that evening Verna said, "Hope that woman sorts out her life. I wonder why she came to us, surely someone like her would have loads of family and friends to help her out."

"Don't be cruel, young lady; she's a troubled woman. I like her; she doesn't have airs and graces."

"Ma, she's nice to us because she's clearly the poor side of that family. If she was rich like Rose, Dawn or Arlene, she won't have given us the time of day, she's just feeling sorry for herself."

"Sometimes I wonder if you're my daughter, you don't seem to have much sympathy for unfortunate people and Priscilla's one such."

"Really, mother! Didn't I go to Bequia to try to sort out something for Arlene's abandoned staff? I reserve my sympathy for those in real need, destitute people with no one to help or care for them, not for people who have rich relatives to help them out when things go 'belly-up' for them. You can't see it, but Priscilla's a user."

Rhoda looked at Verna with shock emanating from her widened eyes and opened mouth. She had felt genuine sympathy for Priscilla, but Verna's words stirred so deeply that she felt a little ashamed that sympathy for Priscilla's predicament had superseded all the anxiety and care she had harboured for Arlene's displaced, poverty-stricken staff. But as hard as she tried, Rhoda couldn't get Priscilla out of her mind and worried if she did find accommodation at some kind-hearted relative's home.

The weeks rolled by without any news of Priscilla, so Rhoda assumed all was well with her and gradually managed to put her to the back of her thoughts. However, one Saturday morning, during her usual quick visit to Hermie's before her market shopping, she heard some new gossip about Arlene's family. Hermie, like all maids, would unintentionally eavesdrop on their employers' conversations and were usually fully aware when there was a family crisis. So, every bit of what she imparted to Rhoda was second-hand and sometimes pure speculation.

Rhoda learnt that Priscilla had returned to town and was staying once again with Beryl and Veronica. Hermie thought Priscilla was an amiable person who had brought a bit of liveliness to the otherwise dull household and was sorry to hear she was returning to Bequia permanently. Rhoda was a little disappointed that after her kindness to Priscilla, even giving up her bed for her, she had ignored them; she felt Verna was right all along, accusing Priscilla of being a 'user'. She left Hermie's filled with confusion but decided she wouldn't say a word to Verna about this new development.

Verna spun the dials on the large cumbersome electric radio to the newly launched WIBS, 'Windward Islands Broadcasting Station', only to hear the soft soulful sounds of Otis Redding singing the ' The Dock of the Bay' which wafted sweetly around the house. She sat down on an easy chair, closed her eyes, allowing herself to imagine being in America and hearing all the great black singers who dominated the West Indies radio waves do their stuff in person.

Urgent knocking at the front door interrupted her relaxation and sweet daydreams. She sucked her teeth and looked towards the back door, to see if Rhoda was near-by to answer the door but she was in the backyard taking dried clothes off the clothesline before the darkening day became night. She reluctantly got up and went to the door. The shock of seeing Priscilla was so profound that for a few seconds no words came out of her opened month.

"Hello Verna, how are you keeping? Just came to say bye before I go home tomorrow," said Priscilla cheerfully.

"Oh, I thought you went back home ages ago," she said a little sarcastically.

She invited the visitor in; Rhoda joined them, and they all sat down. Priscilla was offered a cold lemonade drink, then she was asked why she didn't get in touch with them before when she was still on the island for such a long time.

Priscilla, quite sober than the other times they had encountered her, became tongue-tied but began explaining that she had been living with relatives up the 'hill', referring to Dorsetshire Hill about Kingstown, and had no intention of staying so long there but felt trapped without money or transport means. She eventually was summoned back to Kingstown to talk over her future with her aunts, who really weren't her aunts at all but distant cousins. She said she was prevented from going anywhere and doing anything, then Beryl insisted she return to Carl and give the marriage another try. She was disinclined to do so but realised that she was as lonely among family here as she was in Bequia.

Verna wasn't impressed and took everything that came out of Priscilla's mouth with a pinch of salt. Clearly, she thought, being among some starchy family members kept her from drinking too much, but back in Bequia with a drunk for a husband, she could fill her lonely body with an array of potent alcoholic spirits unrestrained. Rhoda was sympathetic and gave her the benefit of the doubt. The usually jolly drunken person was timidly sober, and they could see she was squirming with embarrassment. However, Rhoda had to concede that Priscilla had plenty of time to contact them, and pretending she was little more than a prisoner was disingenuous.

Herman

Another knock at the door interrupted the discourse; Verna answered it. A sheepish-looking young man about her age asked if Priscilla was there because he came to fetch her.

"Yes, she's here." Her heart skipped a beat; she moved aside to let him in.

"Oh, I must be going; this is my cousin Celia's godson, Herman; he's going to take me to Vermont to see some friends there. I promised to visit them before I return home." She introduced the young man to the ladies. "This is Verna and her mother Rhoda."

"Pleased to meet you, Herman," said Rhoda.

The young man weakly shook Rhoda's hand and then Verna's; he was invited to sit down, but Priscilla jumped up off her chair, signalling they had to leave. At the door, as they were leaving the house, Rhoda asked Herman if he was local.

"No, Miss," said the well-spoken Herman in a soft whisper, "I'm from Stubbs but live with my uncle in Calliaqua."

"He's a civil servant," chipped in Priscilla.

"And you got a car." Rhoda chuckled.

"It's my uncle's car; I'm not that rich yet." He looked at Verna smiling – the warmest smile she ever saw on a man's face, one that said, I'm free.

"What do you make of all that, Ma? Is Priscilla trustworthy, or is she playing us for fools?" asked Verna after Priscilla and Herman left their house.

"Don't know, but I think she's troubled, and the lack of money has her in a bind. She clearly wanted to stay over here but had no choice but to return to a failing marriage and interminable boredom, poor lady."

"And, drink!"

"Unfortunately, once she's back to the boredom, her thirst for drink would be unquenchable."

"Ma, stop wasting pity on her; if she was as rich as Arlene, do you think she would give us the time of day? She's friendly because she doesn't have any friends, and she's beholden to her rich cousins."

"Don't be so harsh; I think she would be a nicer, kinder person without all that baggage, and anyway, isn't Arlene friendly to both of us when she doesn't have to?"

"Ah, yes, but look how she treated us since she moved to England – not a word until she wanted us to lay off her staff. That's them exactly!" Verna was convinced that where poor people were concerned, rich people were untrustworthy.

After supper, Rhoda went to her tabletop sewing machine to finish off a skirt she was making, and Verna settled down with another intriguing book before they retired to bed. By Monday, all was back to normal and Rhoda and her daughter resumed their quiet lives.

Meanwhile, Herman couldn't get Verna out of his mind, and for the first time in the three years since he started to work in accounts at the country's main post office, he made a mistake.

"Noo," he cried out.

"What you do, boy, be careful!" warned his manager.

"It's OK, Mr Richards, no worries!"

"Go, take a break before you bankrupt the post office," Mr Richards ordered.

Herman crossed Back Street from where the post office is located, walked down the side street, and crossed Middle Street before arriving on Bay Street and the seafront. He stood awkwardly on the edge of the road near the beach, scanning the sea with flecks of white water dancing on the surface, signalling the approach of strong winds. Further along the coast, work on the deep-water harbour was feverishly coming to an end. He wasn't taking in the picturesque tableau in front of him; he was thinking of Verna.

He tried to clear his head of the goddess he had seen and wanted to know her more. From the moment he saw her, his heart sang, but he wrangled with thoughts that she may already have a man in her life. He felt he was wasting his time dreaming of her but found it impossible getting her out of his head. So he began to contrive ways he could accidentally bump into her.

Go for a walk along River Road, or be brave and go straight to her home, knock on her door, and ask her out. But of course, he couldn't do that and slowly settled back into his humdrum life with nothing much to do after work but lime with friends. During all that time, Verna was also carrying on her own unchanging life with nothing more to do than work, church and, in the female sense, lime with her friends. Any man who took a shine to her was quickly rebuffed; she just didn't feel he was the right one for her.

Arlene and Sidney finally returned from England and stayed a few days in Kingstown before returning home to Bequia. Rhoda and Verna had had no news of her for such a long time that they assumed they were still abroad. It was just after lunch when she knocked on their door. The ladies were flabbergasted, and neither said anything for a few moments.

"Hello, I'm back!" she greeted them with smiles and open

arms.

"Good to see you, Arlene; never thought we'd see you again," said Rhoda.

Verna just stared and seemed unable to make up her mind whether she was happy to see Arlene or irritated by her unannounced intrusion into their lives again. Rhoda did the talking and asked questions; Arlene answered honestly then turned her full attention to Verna.

"So, how are things with you, Verna? Found a nice fellow yet?"

"I'm doing OK, no complaints and no, haven't found 'Mr Right' yet, still waiting. Are you back for good then?" she asked flatly.

"Yes, back for good; I had enough as soon as I arrived. It's such a dull place, but I stayed for Sidney's sake; he knew I was itching to come home, but he had promised his cousin he'd oversee his business while he was unwell. Glad to say he's better now and back seeing to his business himself. Oh, you have no idea how much I missed the sun, the sea and my family and friends." She pointed her arm in their direction to emphasise that they were included in that list of 'misses'. Before she exited the house, Arlene implored Verna to visit her in Bequia and to be her guest for as long as she liked. Verna promised, but as soon as Arlene left, she regretted that decision.

"That's nice of her inviting you over; she's a really lovely person," said her mother.

"I won't be going, of course; imagine staying as a guest at the very house you worked in as a maid and having to face the same staff you once worked with. I couldn't humiliate them like that; couldn't face Elisha and poor old Bernice." She felt a stab of pity for the impoverished staff.

"But how will you get out of that one? I can't imagine they'd have the same staff; there'll be changes; Bernice's too old, and surely Elisha will have a new job by now. Anyway, if I were you, I'd go and be nice to the staff, chat with them and let them see you're not pretentious. I'm sure they'll be happy to see you." Rhoda hoped her words would inspire Verna.

"Unless she was really lucky, I can't see Elisha obtaining another job in that crowded market; there are a lot of poor women always looking for work. And Arlene won't be happy with her guests fraternising with the staff; they have strict rules about these things. No, it would be too awkward; I shan't go no matter how much she begs; I won't be part of her games." Verna set her face in that determined way that Rhoda hated.

Verna was always happy when there were no distractions in her cosy little world; however, she was still praying for some nice young man to come her way. No one met with her approval, and some said she was too fussy, but she did think Herman looked presentable and wondered why she never saw him again even though he worked at the post office in the middle of town.

On August bank holiday Monday, Verna joined a group of friends and work colleagues for a picnic with bathing on Villa Beach; some said it was the best beach on St Vincent. They were having a great time lolling about on the hot, bronze sand, chatting, laughing, swimming or rather bobbing about in the calm, salty water. They were not the only people on the beach that day, and much to the ladies' chagrin, there were many irritatingly hyperactive children there as well. The ladies did not want their hair getting wet and had a hard time keeping away from the rowdy kids who were splashing about with carefree abandon.

It was late afternoon, the sun was fast dipping into the

horizon, children were being rounded up, empty picnics gathered and people were departing quickly from the beach before darkness fell. Verna and her group were also leaving, walking slowly along towards the beach exit, when a man came up behind her and touched her arm, startling her.

"Verna, my goodness, haven't seen you for ages. I thought you went back to Bequia." It was Calver, half dressed and looking manly and handsome.

"Calver, where did you disappear? I tried looking for you at the club, and no one knew where you went," she said breathlessly, amazed that she had not seen him before on the small, narrow beach.

Before he answered, a lady joined them and took hold of Calver's arm. Verna's enthusiasm evaporated. The lady was his wife, he explained, and she was expecting, as everyone could clearly see. She congratulated them with the broadest of smiles but her heart was in pieces. She bade them farewell and ran off to join her departing friends.

"You know that man?" asked Ruby, a friend and colleague.

"Not really; I saw him bartending at a country club once or maybe twice. He remembered me perhaps because I was the only black girl among all those rich white people he was serving at the time," replied Verna, pretending to be unruffled.

"Well, he's well and truly hooked; his lady's expecting," another friend observed.

Verna didn't reply; she just wished they would shut up, and soon they stood beside the main road, waiting for their prearranged lift back to town. After a while, with the sun almost gone from the day and darkness falling menacingly, the ladies began to feel abandoned.

"Ruby, did you tell your brother to pick us up here?" Selma

asked.

"I did, but he's a bit wayward. I just hope he remembered," replied Ruby, embarrassed.

"Where did he picnic then, on the moon?" asked another. "He should have been here by now.

"Well, I live in Arnos Vale, so I'm walking; I don't want to be standing here in the dark. See you all tomorrow, bye," another said before she and a couple of others walked off.

The group dwindled as most opted to walk to their respected homes in Arnos Vale, Sion Hill and Frenches, east of Kingstown. Eventually, the others who had further to go in Kingstown and surrounding areas – Ruby and Selma to Kingstown Park, Joyce to Rose Place, and Verna to River Road – followed suit. Darkness was obscuring their way on the poorly lit meandering highway; they felt anxious having to share the narrow road without proper sidewalks with the hurrying but thankfully thinly scattered traffic. Those were the days before the regular vans or bus services dashing around the island in sporadic frequency but which, however, would have got them home quickly.

The four of them had just arrived at Arnos Vale with the airport in sight when a car whizzed past them.

"Road hog," screamed Ruby, "the fool could have killed us."

The car turned down a narrow road, and out of sight, the friends continued towards the airport, where they would cross over before climbing the steep hill towards Sion Hill, then Kingstown on the other side. After a few minutes, the car came back and screeched to a stop in front of the young women, its bright headlights blinding them. They cringed and quickly moved aside to allow the mad driver room on the narrow road.

"Can I give you a lift?" asked the young man, popping his head out the window.

Ruby, the feistiest of the lot, shouted at him for putting the fear of God into them and called the others to continue their journey.

As they hurried on, he jumped out of the car and ran after them, apologising. Verna stopped and looked at him.

"Do I know you?" she asked.

"Yes, Miss, I came to your house in Kingstown to collect Miss Priscilla," he replied.

"Ahh, I remember. Your name's Herman, isn't it?"

"Yes. That's why I stopped; I recognised you!" he said breathlessly.

Ruby was getting impatient and tapped her foot agitatedly on the smooth asphalt-paved road. She was on the verge of demanding to know what was going on with the chatty couple in front of her when Herman offered them all a lift to their homes. They accepted. At Verna's, the others having already dropped off, she gathered up her picnic things and exited the car in her usual elegant way. She thanked Herman for his kindness and for coming out of his way.

"That's OK; I was on an errand for my uncle anyway. He's a tailor; I'm going to Cane Garden to pick up a suit for alteration."

"Hope you don't get in trouble with your uncle."

"He won't know anything unless, of course, you blabbed." He giggled.

They giggled like excited children, then he rushed around to open Verna's front door for her. She thanked him, but before she entered the house, he asked her for a date. She scanned him through the dimness of the early evening, her eyes critically moving up and down his toned body, *not too skinny not too muscular, just right,* she thought and with a twinkle, she nodded acceptance. Herman laughed and asked if he could come over at the weekend. She shrugged her shoulders, smiled, closed the door, and left him staring open-mouthed at the door. Verna didn't want to be overly optimistic, but she felt as though she was walking on air.

Herman drove away with a pounding heart and enveloped in a strange, warm and calming glow. The following weekend, the besotted young man called on Verna, surprising Rhoda, who wasn't aware of his interest in her daughter. He arrived on foot, and from that moment Verna understood that he was as poor as she was; she didn't care because she was sure that at last the right man had entered her life.

After two years together, when Verna had just turned twenty-seven and Herman was a confident thirty-year-old, the couple married in the Anglican Cathedral in Kingstown on a cloudless, sweetly breezy Saturday morning. It wasn't a flashy affair, only the two families, which weren't many people anyway, a few friends and some co-workers from both couple's offices, and of course, Arlene, without Sidney. The reception wasn't elaborate, just consisting of a lovely luncheon, which was held at a hotel on Bay Street and which was paid for by Arlene as a wedding gift. There wasn't much of a honeymoon either, just a few days on Mayron at Herman's insistence because he wanted to know the place his wife came from and he had never been to the Grenadines before.

Herman fell in love with Mayron as deeply as he did with Verna. He enjoyed the flat, almost desert-like scenarios, the wide silver sand beaches, the calm, shallow bathing and the friendliness of the thinly dispersed population. There was a wonderful simplicity to the place; even the tiny room they slept in at the home of one of Rhoda's friends was magical to him.

Instead of concentrating on Verna, he insisted that they visited every corner of the tiny island and that she introduced him to all the people she knew, which was about everyone. She began to feel a little uneasy; it looked as though her husband was falling in love with the tiny isle, openly proclaiming that he'd rather live there than the place they depended on for their livelihood.

Once they were back from their brief honeymoon, they moved into the River Road house, sharing residency with Rhoda. But as the months rolled by, Rhoda began to feel uncomfortable with the housing arrangement. She felt the young couple should be on their own and began to feel like an interloper in the small house. Unknown to them, she began looking for alternate accommodation for herself. With her small wages, she couldn't afford anything as good as the River Road residence.

She pondered that she would have to become a lodger again, but even that would be too expensive. She was in a bind but refused to demean herself by moving into something like Hermie's that could only be called a slum. She continued living with the couple, and the three of them made the best of it. She was pleased Herman and her daughter were getting along really well but felt there was a muted atmosphere because of her presence.

On Saturday evenings after supper, if they had nothing better to do, such as a trip to the cinema, they would all be sitting in the living room in semi-darkness listening to a random Latin American radio station's uninterrupted sweet Merengue beat. Verna would be tapping her feet to the music and imagining the senoritas swirling on the dance floor with their full skirts swishing around romantically in all directions. She waited patiently for her pensive husband to swing her wildly or hold her closely to the intoxicating Latin melody. Instead, his thoughts were far away from music and dance; they were churning over with the prospects of business and money-making. He spoilt the atmosphere one such evening by turning the radio down and making a startling suggestion.

"I was thinking a lot about Mayron; I would like to set up a general store over there selling everything under one roof, like the big ones here. There was hardly anything much there; it could be a really nice store catering for everyone."

He waited for his idea to sink in; the reaction was shock on the ladies' faces. Rhoda and Verna looked at each other; neither found words to express the potential of moving back to their tiny home island.

"Well, what do you think?" he asked no one in particular.

Rhoda was the first to find her voice. "You see Mayron as a tourist, Herman, beautiful and unspoilt, but living there is another thing; it could be a real challenge" – she turned to Verna – "remember the poverty, the struggle and how you had to leave home so young to make a living?"

"I remember! It's a truly beautiful little place, second to none, I'd say, but it's hard work for poor people." A few tears rolled down her cheeks, dripping onto her lap as she remembered her carefree childhood and having to leave home so young.

Herman was taken aback by the ladies' reaction; he had hoped his idea would be enthusiastically welcomed. He thought Mayron would be a new start for them and hadn't given much consideration as to why the ladies left their idyllic homeland in the first place.

"Do you really think a store would make enough money to live comfortably in such a small place with a mostly poor population? Didn't you say your uncle was struggling over in Calliaqua, making just enough to get by? And there are more people living there than on Mayron. And what about the couple of stores already there? You'd put them out of business for sure," said Verna sadly.

"But Uncle has a lot of competition; people buy ready-made these days; tailors are few and far between now. People seem to use tailors only for formal suits these days, but mainly just for alterations and repairs. Those like my uncle do struggle, but the bigger ones, like here in Kingstown, do really well," said Herman like a man who knew his subject.

"So, you think a store would succeed on Mayron, and we would make enough to afford our own home to support a family plus paying school fees and accommodation for higher education over here. Also, how are you going to finance it?" asked Verna.

"Borrow money from the bank, of course. I'm an accountant; I know how to manoeuvre money," he replied confidently.

"So, with no collateral but only a money-making idea, the bank will hand money over to you. I think you should ask them first, and if they agree, we'd give it a go." Verna was warming to the idea faster than she realised.

Rhoda was horrified! It would mean years of struggle for the couple, and her recollection of her family's long-enduring poverty on the tiny island filled her with apprehension. Herman was smart and full of ideas, but she couldn't see him making even fair money, especially with the competition already there.

"Well, Ma, what do you think?" asked Verna, brightening up every second to her husband's ideas.

"It's your life; you'd have to make that decision yourself. If you're really serious, Herman, go back to Mayron and survey the place with the eyes of a businessman and not a tourist; talk to the locals to see what they'd like to have that they hadn't got now; then maybe you'd have a viable project," said his smart mother-in-law.

"I saw a beautiful paradise and wished to live there forever with my wife, but I've forgotten there's always a flip side. Anyway, I'd talk to the bank and see what they think. True, I don't have collateral, but banks are known to trust people with good entrepreneurial ideas. Let's hope they like mine." Herman smiled at his wife, knowing he had her full support.

"Though I swore I would never live back there again, I think you've a great idea, and I'm with you all the way." With a smile on her face, Verna crossed her fingers.

Six months later, the Mayron adventure was put to bed. The banks poured scorn on Herman's idea, and he gave up on his dream. The place and population, they said, were too small to make a sustainable profit, and there was a median-sized store there already, which would diminish any budding profit.

However, one financial adviser, Herman, asked for ideas, suggesting the couple should look into the hotel business because the Grenadines were getting quite popular with international tourists. He pointed out that Mustique was already popular with royalty and the super rich, and the same good fortune could spread to the other islands. The couple couldn't see tourists flocking to an almost inaccessible island in the lower Grenadines and so thought that was not a good idea.

"I never saw tourists flocking to Mayron when I was growing up except the odd yacht stopping over for repairs. They went to Bequia, but mostly to Mustique; perhaps years from now Mayron would join the tourist age, but that would be too late for us," Verna surmised.

"I don't want to be a hotelier anyway; I have no idea how that works. Well, no harm in dreaming," said Herman, sad that his dreams were in tatters.

Not long afterwards, Verna found she was expecting a baby, which coincided with the couple moving into a newly built three-bedroom house in the fast-growing suburb of New Montrose. This modern house was built for another family who suddenly fell on hard times through illness and had to sell their long-hoped-for home. Herman heard of the family's misfortune through a colleague, and though one of the banks he had approached before turned down his Mayron ambitions, they were happy to give him a mortgage for the New Montrose house.

Though the approach to the house was a little steep, it rested on the gradual rising hilly area north-west of the capital, and it was situated above a narrow winding road. To afford to live in New Montrose with its colourful brick-built homes showed that the family belonged to the growing educated and financially viable middle class, which Herman and Verna were suddenly thrust into.

They were pleased with their modern home with its internal bathroom facilities, its fitted kitchen with a large stove, and an American-style two-door refrigerator. They adored their home's elevated and desirable position from where they could see the whole of the capital beneath them and Bequia with the smoky outlines of some Grenadine islands on the horizon.

Rhoda's Independence

Rhoda couldn't be happier for her daughter; whenever she visited, she would sit by the window, taking in the view. She would smile with contentment, proud of what her child had achieved, and waited expectantly for her grandchild to arrive.

"You all right in River Road, Ma? You know you can move

in here with us; there's room," said the heavily pregnant Verna, anxious about her mother being alone in her River Road home.

"I know you're happy to have me here, darling, but I think it's best I stayed in River Road, and besides, I got a boarder," said Rhoda.

"You got a boarder, how, when?"

"A school girl. You know how gossipy the church ladies are. Well, one of them said country people are always looking for good homes for their children to board when they come to town to attend the high schools. Someone suggested I could help because I had the room now you and Herman had moved on."

"What sauce! It's none of their business!"

"I know, but gossip spreads fast here, and anyway, they guessed my situation. I don't own my home, and I don't get the kind of wages to enable me to live in a decent two-bed house alone. A young girl called Yvonne is coming soon to live with me."

Rhoda didn't tell her daughter that she got lonely, especially at night, that she didn't enjoy cooking for one, and that she really missed her. Verna was glad her mother would have company and knew the child would be well cared for. Deep down, she hoped her mother would reside with them but was aware that her mother had become independent and she didn't want to intrude. But it was only a short walk away from River Road, and Rhoda had promised she would help with the baby whenever she could; it looked like she would be spending a great deal of time at New Montrose.

A lovely little girl was born to Verna and Herman at the Kingstown General Hospital's, and when they were discharged a few days later, Verna, at one point, found it a bit tedious with the regular stream of visitors. One of the first to visit was Arlene, who showed her love for Verna by coming over from Bequia as soon as she was told the news via a telephone call from her mother. She came laden with gifts for the couple and their baby, who was the recipient of countless little nighties, rompers, nappies and toys she couldn't play with until she was at least two years old.

Thereafter, whenever Arlene came over to visit her mother, she would turn up unannounced to see Verna and the baby. When the time came for baby Estelle to be christened, before Arlene could ask, as she had intended to, the couple asked her to be godmother. She was elated, and from that moment on she behaved as though she were the grandmother, and sometimes Rhoda felt put out. Verna fulfilled all her roles: wife, mother, housewife and office worker without the slightest hint of dissent. With her mother's help babysitting and that of a middle-aged 'home-helper', she refused to use the term domestic; she was able to return to work quickly.

Herman would have preferred it if Verna had become a permanent housewife, but she returned to work only a few weeks after having baby Estelle. This allowed them to keep the standard of living they had gotten used to; less money coming in would have meant slipping backwards, and though they had to be careful, she didn't want her child to experience the poverty of her parents' childhood. If it was one thing that she craved more above all others, was her child attending a good primary school, then a high school. So, when Arlene came up with the idea of sending Estelle to a fee-paying preparatory school when she turned five, Verna was elated and ready to take up the offer. However, when she told Herman of Arlene's wonderful plan, he became incensed. He had been grateful for all Arlene had done for them, such as the wedding reception and numerous gifts since, but he thought her interference had gone too far.

"I'll pay for my child's education when the time comes; I don't want the rich lady's charity," he said, his voice trembling with anger.

"She's only trying to help; she's been kind to us," said Verna, forgetting the times before she married when she viewed Arlene's interference with resentment.

Herman knew their salaries covering the mortgage and living expenses couldn't stretch to a fee-paying school yet, but he was certain the promotion he was after at the post office would enable Estelle to attend a high school when the time came. She would have to start off at a government primary school just like her parents had done, and he hoped she would do better than they did. He had obtained a scholarship to the fee-paying Boys Grammar School and had passed all his school leaving certificates, then acquired a scholarship to the University of the West Indies.

These worries about Estelle's future were temporarily put on hold for a while as life continued for the new family smoothly and happily. Everyone seemed to be thriving, and Rhoda said it was her prayers being answered; she had a boarder, her job, her church, quite a few friends, and a growing family. But her peaceful life was abruptly interrupted one morning after breakfast when Hermie's son Byron was sent to fetch her to go to Beryl Lorraine's home. She didn't ask why she was needed but thanked the young man, then left her home, walking as fast as she could to see what she could do for the ailing, fragile Beryl. She knocked at the front door, which surprisingly was opened by Veronica and not a maid.

"Thanks for coming; the doctor's upstairs; it's bad; she doesn't look good," said Veronica, visibly shaking and red-eyed.

Rhoda raced upstairs to Beryl's room to see the doctor gently moving his stethoscope around Beryl's concave chest; his patient lay pale and still. Rhoda moved to the other side of the large bed, stretched across to hold Beryl's skeletal hand.

"All we can do now is comfort her to the end," said the elderly Dr Masterson. "I've sent for Arlene; hope she gets here in time."

"What happened? I visited a couple of days ago; she seemed lively, chatting away as usual." Rhoda was puzzled about Beryl's rapid deterioration.

"As you know," said Dr Masterson, an old family friend of the old ladies and who had seen Rhoda visiting, "she had many problems; her body just gave up; a nurse would be here soon. Would you stay with her till then?"

"Yes, yes, doctor, don't worry, I'll stay right here till the nurse comes."

He put his stethoscope and other medical paraphernalia he had on the bedside table into his large black bag, nodded to Rhoda, and left. She wiped Beryl's feverish brow with a damp flannel cloth, adjusted the thin sheet covering her cadaverous body, and then Veronica entered the room.

"Just after breakfast, my poor sister was sitting in her chair chatting with me when she keeled over. Ricky, that is, Dr Masterson, said it's possibly a stroke. Arlene should be here sometime this afternoon; I hope she makes it in time. I can't bear it!" She howled and hurried from the room. When the nurse arrived, Rhoda left and walked as fast as she could up to New Montrose to tell Verna the news. They all knew Beryl was ailing, but her imminent demise was more sudden than they had foreseen.

Early that evening, just after Arlene and Sidney's arrival,

Beryl passed away. After supper with her child boarder, Rhoda retreated to the kitchen, doing the washing up and tidying up. The child sat at the dining table doing her homework when there was a knock at the door. To Rhoda's amazement, it was Veronica standing at the door. She had never been to the River Road house before and maybe never wandered the streets of Kingstown alone in the dark, either.

It never occurred to Rhoda to invite the sisters to her tiny home, even though she was a regular visitor to their substantial one. Arlene had arranged for her and Verna to call on her mother and aunt to keep them company sometimes, but only Rhoda fulfilled that role. She had wondered if Veronica was happy with her being in their home because she never participated in the lively conversations she had had with Beryl. Mostly, as Rhoda entered, Veronica left the room, perhaps signalling that she was not comfortable in her presence.

It was a dark night. The clouds were heavily obscuring the moon into a thin, pale crescent shape. Veronica looked ghostly against the dark backdrop of the night, her heavily lined face etched with deep sorrow. Rhoda stretched out to the old lady, gently pulling her into her brightly lit living room.

"I guess it's over. She's at rest now, gone to the angels," Rhoda rightly guessed.

"Yes, it happened around five, she simply slipped away when no one was looking. I've lived with her and Dicky since Arlene was a little girl, then Dicky died – too young – and she and I have been inseparable; I'll miss her terribly." She turned her tear-splattered face towards Rhoda and asked, "What's going to happen to me now?"

Rhoda had no answer but sympathised; she had never noticed before how frail Veronica looked. She offered her a drink of sherry from a bottle she kept for emergencies; it was gladly accepted. They sat quietly sipping sherry from small. slender glasses before the solitude was interrupted by young Yvonne, saying goodnight as she withdrew to her bedroom.

"Goodnight, dear, sleep tight." Rhoda smiled at Yvonne, then turned her attention back to Veronica. "You better go home; they might be wondering where you are, and it's getting late."

"Arlene knows I'm here; she got Marlene to bring me here. She wanted me out of the house because I was howling too much," she said, feeling a tad uplifted after the alcohol.

"Can you find your way back alone? I can't leave the child now she's in bed."

"I know the way back: down pass the churches, then left towards the town centre. I must brace myself for the funeral; I must endure it for my big sister's sake. You know, she was the best sister in the world; we got along really well. You see, it's childhood; we had a happy one; our parents indulged us too much. Did Beryl ever tell you that we used to swim from Villa Beach to Young Island and back regularly when we were younger? Oh, we were great swimmers. As we got older, we swam less and less, and now I couldn't tell you the last time salt water touched our bodies. That's old age for you!"

"I know what you mean. Verna and I swam a lot back in Mayron, but since being in town we hardly do that any more. We went a few times down in front of the Anglican school on Bay Street, but since Verna got married, none of us have been near the sea."

"What about the child?" Veronica nodded towards the bedroom door she saw Yvonne enter. "You should take her swimming with you; it's good for children."

"You're so right, I'll do just that," replied Rhoda, a little surprised by Veronica's observation.

"Thanks for your company, Rhoda; I feel much better; I must go back now."

She rose gingerly from the chair and began to exit the house with small, careful strides. Rhoda changed her mind. After warning Yvonne not to leave her room or answer the front door, she accompanied the old lady back to her home, making sure she entered safely. When she returned and after checking on Yvonne, she went to bed, but sleep was slow coming, she couldn't get the lonely Veronica out of her mind.

The week whizzed past in a blur. Beryl was buried in the churchyard, and Sidney returned to Bequia, but Arlene remained in Kingstown. Rhoda was glad she didn't have to help out during that tense time; Arlene had it covered, and numerous relatives, including Priscilla, were there to lend a hand. Though Beryl had never spoken of family to Rhoda, except for Arlene, she suspected there were many others, and the attendance at the funeral proved so.

A Chance Meeting

One Sunday afternoon a few weeks later, Rhoda, Verna and Estelle went strolling in the Botanic Gardens. They stopped to admire the large, round pond with its watery surface almost obscure, with green lily leaves languidly covering the still water beneath. Toddler Estelle tried to disentangle herself from the adults' grasp; she wanted to walk on the green shimmery carpet-like display in front of her. After trying to appease the little one and failing, the adults decided to leave the gardens and return home.

As soon as they walked out the high-railed gates, her attention was taken over by passing traffic and other Sunday afternoon strollers. They were quite close to home when a car pulled up almost smack bang in front of them. Verna grabbed her child, Rhoda squirmed, then recovering, she marched to the side of the car to rebuke the driver.

"You fool, you could have killed us; can't you see this is a narrow road, not fit for speeding?" she said, pounding on the driver's door.

"Ah sorry, but ah wasn't speeding; the corner was too sharp," said the trembling young man behind the wheel.

A thin man immaculately dressed in white emerged from the back of the car, apologising profusely for the driver's folly of 'taking' the narrow corner too sharply. Rhoda and her family stomped off in disgust when they were halted by the faint familiarity of the voice.

"My God, Anty Rhoda? It's me, Earl!" He rushed forward to the startled women.

"No, can't be! Earl, where have you been all these years?" Rhoda embraced his thin frame. As recognition washed over her, her eyes filled with tears.

"Wonderful seeing you all again after all these years. Ah can't believe it. Anty, you look lovely. Are you visiting Kingstown?" Then he took a double take of the sight of Verna.

There were more hugs, and Verna asked the men to her home just a few steps away. They sat and chatted while drinking Sorrel and eating home-made sweet bread. There was a lot to catch up on, and Joel kept apologising repeatedly for his poor driving, but he was forgiven. Earl said the car was his, but he couldn't drive, so he needed Joel to ferry him and his family about when required. They were in the capital to collect merchandise from his friend in Middle Street but had decided at the last moment, as they reached New Montrose on their way back home to Layou, to call upon an old, unwell friend who lived further along the road. He couldn't believe his luck, meeting his old friends by chance on a narrow residential street.

Checking the time on his leather strap watch, Earl said, "You all please come to Layou to meet Hannah and the children; how bout next Sunday? We can catch up properly with more time. We've to go back now."

"I'd have to check with Herman first, but I'm sure it'll be OK," said Verna.

"Joel can come pick you up at two o'clock, all right?" he asked.

"OK, we'll see you around two, but Herman will bring us," replied Verna, who didn't trust Joel's driving.

When Earl and Joel departed, the ladies waved from the front steps as the car haltingly jerked away towards Leeward.

"Looks like an old car to me; I won't want to go anywhere in that," said Rhoda.

"It's not brand-new, but I think it's a case of the driver, not the car. He's a bad driver; no wonder Earl was in the back seat; he was scared."

"What's the point of having a car if you can't drive?" said Rhoda as they retreated into the house, tittering. She expressed admiration for Earl, who, once poor and semiliterate, had come so far as to own his own business.

Twilight was fading, being pushed aside by the impatient darkness of night when she returned home just as Yvonne, who was visiting school friends, arrived home as well. Rhoda rushed around preparing their supper, then sat down with Yvonne to eat at the dining table, but she was distracted.

"What!" Yvonne had said something to her.

"Oh, Miss Rhoda, I was asking if you all right? You look sad and far away," said the observant girl.

"Sorry, dear. We had a shock today."

"My goodness, was someone hurt?"

"No, but we were nearly run over by a car near Verna's home."

"Oh my God!" Yvonne put her hand to her mouth, her eyes wide in astonishment.

"Well, he wasn't speeding, but that road is too narrow for people and cars at the same time, it doesn't have a sidewalk. Anyway, no one got hurt, but the shock was that the car belonged to a friend of ours from back home."

"Bequia!"

"No, Yvonne, Mayron; I told you before I'm from Mayron, miles south of Bequia. His name's Earl, and he lives in Layou."

"You mean Earl the barber, that everybody calls 'Slim' cause he's really skinny, like he doesn't eat, so Pappy says. He and my little brother Frankie go to Layou for him to cut their hair."

Rhoda was stunned; all that time Yvonne lived with her, she had never bothered to really get to know the girl. She never once asked her about her life back home in Barrouallie, and all the time the girl was a hive of information. By the time they left the table, Rhoda knew a lot more about her young charge and Earl.

"In a couple of weeks, when I go back home for half-term, we'd probably go to Layou, my mother's, from there. You must visit Barrouallie, Miss Rhoda; it's a lovely place, getting bigger every year."

Rhoda felt a little ashamed that in all the time they lived on the main island, they had never visited any other part of the country they call home – Leeward on the west coast or Windward on the east coast. They went as far as Calliaqua on the Windward side when Herman took them to meet his aunt and uncle and further along to Stubbs to meet his widowed mother, but ventured no further.

She had heard of the Leeward villages of Lowmans, Questelles, Chauncey, Buccament Bay, Layou, Barrouallie and Chateaubelair. And the Windward coastal villages of Biabou, Colonaire and Georgetown, but never felt any curiosity about going to any of those places. Suddenly, she wanted to go and explore and to see why Earl chose Leeward to settle and not the thriving capital. Every time she visited her daughter, Rhoda had new gossip and sometimes good information to impart. She told her all about Yvonne and how informative she was about Earl.

"So, she's from Layou!" remarked Verna.

"No, I said she's from Barrouallie, but her mother originally came from Layou. Apparently to appease his wife, the father and little brother have their hair cut by Earl whenever they go back there. They like Earl or Slim, as he's known, so much they keep going back."

"So, there's no barber in Barrouallie?" asked a puzzled Verna.

"Aren't you listening, girl? They use Earl, not because there isn't a barber in Barrouallie, but because her mother goes back regularly to see her relatives in Layou, and they use Earl's services."

Eventually, when she thought she could get a word in, Verna announced that Herman would take them to see Earl that coming Sunday. She said she couldn't wait to see what Earl had done for himself. Rhoda walked back home with a new perkiness in her steps; she was glad to have Yvonne for company in her house.

She was also proud of her daughter's thriving life, and she couldn't wait to congratulate the boy from Mayron on his accomplishments.

Verna sat in the front passenger seat next to Herman as he drove them in his uncle's car through Leeward. Rhoda and Estelle sat in the back, the child jumping around wanting to see everything they passed on the way there. Rhoda tried to contain her best she could; she was frightened a door might fly open and the child would be dashed to pieces on the highway.

She and Verna cringed at every sharp bend on the narrow road, every steep downward or upward section. Every time the ladies saw people or animals wandering carefree on the highway, they braced themselves and closed their eyes anticipating a collision. But Herman was a careful driver, and he called out the areas they were passing through to give the ladies a sense of place when they recalled the journey in the future: Lowmans, Campden Park, Questelles, Chauncey, Buccament Bay and Layou.

The ladies were glad they arrived unscathed and were impressed with the small village situated on several flat streets quite close to a secluded bay front. Earl's place was two streets from the seafront and tucked away in the far corner facing the sea. He rushed out when the car pulled up, greeting the ladies with hugs, Herman with a firm handshake, and Estelle with a head rub, which she pulled away from. He took them around the back and up the concrete stairs to the family dwelling.

"This is my wife, Hannah." He proudly gave her a gentle shove towards the visitors.

"Pleased to meet you, Hannah," said Rhoda, grabbing the nervous lady's hand.

The visitors sat down on narrow, easy chairs while Earl and Hannah sat on a couple of dining chairs. While drinking cold drinks and nibbling on an array of homemade cakes and sweet breads, they talked of past lives, struggles and where they were at that present time.

"By the way, Earl, did you ever get the letter I sent you from Bequia?" asked Verna.

"What letter? Ah never got no letter from you; from nobody since ah come over. Where did you send it to?" His brow knitted in curiosity.

"The post office. You should go and ask for it; it may still be there somewhere."

She immediately regretted mentioning the letter because she couldn't remember what she had written when she thought Earl would be her liberator from small island boredom all those years ago. She wished she had kept her mouth shut.

"The next time I go to town for supplies, I'll go to the post office and see if they can find it after all this time," he said, feeling like he had won a prize and couldn't wait to collect it.

Herman and Hannah were temporarily forgotten while the other three reminisced. Herman was trying to calm a bored Estelle while Hannah was doing the same with her two small sons, though they were older than Estelle. Earl became irritated by the children's interference and suggested to Hannah to take them out for a walk. Herman gladly took Estelle's hand and followed suit.

"There's a lot to catch up on for those three," Herman said as they walked towards the beach with the children. "Imagine living in such a small country and not bumping into each other before."

"I guess because nobody travels around much. I haven't been to Kingstown for months; I only go to buy things for the children, like shoes and things like that. If we had a good regular bus service, people would move around more and get more acquainted with each other and the country." Hannah sounded surprisingly articulate and smarter than she presented herself; Herman had thought her a little backward.

"So true. Well, now that we know of each other, we should keep in touch more."

"Yes, we should," she said. They arrived at the beach, and the children went wild.

When the others left, Earl took his country folk downstairs to show off his personal care shop and barber salon. Rhoda 'oohed' and 'aahed'. She was genuinely impressed and had to hold back tears when an image of destitute Rosanna and her child flitted through her memory. Rosanna would be so proud of her son who didn't allow poverty to crush him but used it as inspiration to achieve something in his life, she pondered. The ladies weren't as frightened on the journey back home; they had other things occupying their minds. The rise of Earl was remarkable to say the least, and they were happy that they all had achieved something since leaving Mayron.

The following Sunday, before Yvonne went home for half-term to Barrouallie, Rhoda and Verna with Estelle and Yvonne in tow, went for a walk through the Botanic Gardens. Instead of admiring the wonderful plants, trees and flowers, the ladies were too occupied with Earl to take much in. Yvonne walked off in front with Estelle running after her, playing hide and seek between the plants.

"Rosanna's smiling in heaven. She can rest in peace now; her son's done well," said Rhoda, proud of Earl's ascension.

"I suppose so, but it's all a bit rough," said her daughter, seemingly uninterested in Earl's good fortune.

"What do you mean?" asked her mother, puzzled.

"Well, the shop's haphazard, stuff pushed in all over the place, no finesse whatsoever, and the whole house could do with a lick of paint. He should make the place more inviting; it's so country!"

"Verna!" Rhoda stopped in her tracks and was genuinely shocked with her daughter's criticism of a successful, hard-working compatriot. "I can't believe it; you should be proud of what he's done. You've become so uppity."

Verna tried to explain that she hadn't meant to put Earl down but just thought that his shop was overstuffed and uninviting, unlike the well-laid-out stores in the capital. She apologised profusely and tried to reassure her mother that she wasn't jealous of Earl, but only meant to point out a little lack of subtlety with the store's layout. Never before was there an undercurrent between Verna and her mother like the one developing. Rhoda was shocked that her daughter had become a snob like so many town people, looking down on the country folk as uneducated and unsophisticated fools. She found it difficult to forgive Verna for forgetting in such a short time their own impoverished origins.

Arlene came over from Bequia to see how her aunt was coping on her own. Verna was the first person she visited, who told her all about Earl. She said Rhoda now thought of her as an inveterate snob, and she was unable to satisfy her mother with grovelling apologies. Arlene listened with her head cocked like an elderly school mistress, then sympathetically warned that it was best not to comment or interfere in other people's business unless they asked for assistance. She had gone to Verna's expecting a warm welcome and cheerful conversation. However, she endured an hour of vacuous moaning from her otherwise positive young friend.

She said, "Apologise to your mother and reassure her that you were making an observation."

"I tried, but she won't listen. She thinks I should have never commented on Earl's affairs. She's very proud of him doing so well and thinks I should have congratulated his achievements rather than criticise. I'm not sure what to do; I'm afraid I'll lose her; she's very taken with Earl," Verna said sadly.

Rhoda went to Barrouallie with Yvonne for a few days during the schools' half-term holidays. Verna saw them leave that afternoon on a small, crowded launch from the jetty they knew so well. It was a bright, hot day with a cloudless sky, the sea flat calm, and there wasn't even a hint of breeze, but the loud chug-chugging of the motor made her feel a little anxious. She hoped they got safely to their destination when the boat slowly motored out of the harbour and out of sight around Edinboro Hill, moving up the Leeward coast. She wondered if going by boat was less hazardous than a nail-biting journey on a cumbersome bus on steep, narrow roads.

Somehow, she and her mother had put all the bad feelings behind them, and things had gotten back to a sort of normality. She felt a pang of jealousy that her mother was going to be with Earl when she heard Yvonne's family spend a lot of time between Layou and Barrouallie. However, she decided to behave like the grownup she was and concentrate on her own family. Never mind Earl, she reflected, I have the two most important people in the world at my side, Herman and Estelle.

While Rhoda was away, Verna and Arlene became close again and spent every spare moment in each other's company. There wasn't any clubbing and drinking of strong drinks any more but visits to each other's homes and strolls with Estelle whenever possible. Verna felt relaxed in the reassuring older woman's company, and even Herman noticed a spring in her step and a brightness in her demeanour in Arlene's company. Arlene didn't want to go back home; she wanted to be close to Verna and Estelle, but Sidney needed her as well. She wanted to help the couple; she wanted to give them something big and lasting; she didn't want Verna to ever forget her.

Chapter 7

Fulfilment

It was the first time Rhoda actually took time to see the beauty of her adopted island, and she was amazed at how relaxed she felt exploring the far country. When Yvonne's father Felix took her, in his little motor boat, further up the coast to visit Chateaubelair, she fell in love with the village, immediately likening its remoteness to her native Mayron. She romantically considered moving to that far-flung place permanently one day. This unspoilt peaceful seaside village reminded her so much of Mayron, except that the sand on the beach was not shining silver crystals but more like fine black beads. However, the feel on bare feet was exactly the same – a soft, scorching hotness.

Rhoda returned alone from her Leeward trip, absolutely full of zest; Yvonne would be away for another week. She stood patiently waiting opposite the police station in front of the jetty for Herman to collect her and her many raffia baskets surrounding her on the sidewalk. She was laden with goodies for herself and her daughter's family. She brought with her ducana, a steamed delicacy made from the root vegetable tannia, sweet potatoes and grated coconut, neatly folded into 'banana leaves' and tied with string.

In one of her baskets there was an unusually large bag of farine, which was a white grainy floury seasonal foodstuff and which she had bought from time to time in the market. And best of all, wrapped in brown paper was salted blackfish, which was a small whale species caught mainly off Barrouallie waters. It reminded her of her childhood and hearing the exciting news that a large whale was caught off Bequia by local 'whalemen' which meant that all the Grenadines, including Mayron, would benefit from a large ingestion of healthy whale meat.

She was impressed that Felix and his family were well-known growers of the cassava plants that the farine was subsequently manufactured from. She loved eating the mashed avocado and farine mixture or stirring condensed milk in it to eat as breakfast porridge. Her heart was full of renewed love for St Vincent and the Grenadines after her brief stay in this far-off corner of Leeward. She was full of enthusiasm when talking to her family about the island's rugged beauty and said she wanted to see more, not only in Leeward but on the Windward side as well. With Estelle on her lap while sitting in front of the 'viewing window' she called the front room window she often sat at, she talked non-stop; the others were unable to get a word in.

"Did you know that Chateaubelair is quite close to La Soufriere, the volcano? It's going to erupt sometime soon, and I'd like to see it before it erupts and blows us all to kingdom come. It's very close to Chateaubelaire and the Caribbean country in the north. I'd love to go there one day. You know Verna, I think we have Carib blood in us," she declared.

Herman chipped in, "I climbed the volcano!"

"Really! When was that?" asked his wife, ignoring her mother's declaration.

"Oh, when I was at school. The year before I left, a group of us and a master climbed the magnificent mountain, and I'll never forget that experience."

"Was it a hard climb? Did it take all day?"

"Guess being young and strong and it being more a walk up rather than a climb, I didn't find it too taxing, but a girl with us fainted and a boy vomited when we arrived at the summit. After all, it's over four thousand feet high, and you begin to feel lightheaded as you get closer to the top, but when you get there, what a view! Magnificent!" Herman gushed.

"Perhaps too much for me at my age now, but I'd still love to visit the Caribbean country," said Rhoda.

"Ma, I don't think we have any indigenous blood in us; we're mainly black with a touch of English and French, hence our colouring." Verna tried to correct her excited mother.

"Who told you that? There must be indigenous people in us; my mother told me when I was little that Caribs used to live in all the islands before they were turfed off by the English, who replaced them with African slaves," said Rhoda, proud of her family's ancestry.

"We learnt in school that the slave owners didn't allow the yellow-skinned indigenous people to intermingle with the slaves because they were afraid the two sides would revolt and wipe them out. But escaped slaves did have liaisons, and eventually there were more mixed Caribs than pure ones. Some Vincentians have Carib blood, but the purer-blooded ones were forced to live in their designated northern reservation." Herman was proud of his history lesson to the ladies.

"Poor people, pushed around on their own land and forced to live on a reservation," said Rhoda, shaking her head in sorrow.

"But what of the poor slaves? They had a harder time of it. Brought to a strange country, forced to give up their names, language and culture. Families split asunder and brutally forced to work, from tiny children to old people; every day of their lives from morning till night, they were the 'Poor' people!" Verna said passionately.

"How do you know all of that?" asked her mother.

"Oh, in school. Mrs Calder told us the slaves worked so hard most were dead before they got to thirty. Could you imagine the hardship they were under? The English tried to get the Caribs to work, but they fought back, so they banished them from all the islands and sent most of them to Belize in Central America, and the few remaining were herded in the north on a reservation. Horrible!"

"How come I never heard of such things? I know of slavery but not the details; anyway, I don't want to hear any more about my ancestors' sufferings," said Rhoda, chastened.

"The older people won't talk of the bad old days because I think it hurts too much; that is why our parents and grandparents never discussed slavery with us. It's done and dusted now, and what we must do is never allow anyone to force us into that sort of servitude again. We must move on, but never forget!"

"I agree. Herman, would you take us to see more of the island one day?" asked his wife.

"OK, it's a promise we can go to bathe in the Salt Pond at Owia up in the Caribbean country, then we can do some more exploring of the entire area. A friend of mine's family originally came from Fancy, right at the very top of the island, so I won't mind going there."

Herman then went on to describe getting there via Georgetown, St Vincent's second town, and crossing the Rabacca Dry River with its unpredictable shifting meandering soft bed, which separates the extreme north eastern area of the island from the rest of the country.

"I heard of Salt Pond; some of the girls at work said that they went there once. They said the journey to get to it was quite harrowing – steep hills and rough roads – and even though they liked the experience of swimming in the natural pool made by the Atlantic, they said they won't be doing that again," said Verna wistfully.

The House

Five years after her mother's death, Arlene announced that she had built a beautiful house on Cane Garden at a site on the promontory that gave panoramic views of Bequia and a hazy outline of some Grenadine islands, straggling both the Atlantic Ocean and Caribbean Sea. None of the others knew of the house or Arlene's plans, so it was a total shock to everyone when she announced it was finished and she wanted them to come with her to view it.

Herman eased his recently purchased second-hand car with its occupants, Arlene, Rhoda, Verna and Estelle, onto the wide driveway in front of the large newly built house.

Rhoda exclaimed, "Oh, my goodness, Bequia so close!"

They all exited the car with eyes glued to the wonderful site of the Grenadines stretching out into the dark blue sea, busy with flecks of white water on the Atlantic Ocean's side and darkly calm on the Caribbean Sea's side.

Herman stooped down to Estelle's level and pointed to the islands.

"Your mother came from over there," he said, "one day we'll all go there for a visit."

"It's close; can we swim to that one, Daddy?" asked the confused child before Rhoda pointed something else out to her.

"Look, Estelle, see that boat going towards Bequia? It's one of the many ferries going between St Vincent and the Grenadines. One day we'll go on one of those to visit Mayron, where your mother and I came from."

"Where is Mayron? Is it that one behind Bequia?" The child's eyes sparkled with wonder.

"No," chipped in Arlene, "that's Mustique; Mayron is further down the islands, and it's smaller than Mustique and Bequia; in fact, it's the smallest of all the inhabited islands. Anyway, we're here to see this house. Come in, everyone."

From the gallery adjoining the living room, they were stunned with the views of the capital nestled beneath and its surrounding hills on all sides. Its sheltered calm harbour waters lapping on its dark shores further along the capital's front and closer to them, the newly finished deep-water harbour making the capital look large and business-like.

"The view is magnificent, and this is a beautiful house, Arlene. Are you and your husband going to live here?" asked Rhoda.

"No and yes. We've built a house on Dorsetshire Hill, where Aunt Veronica will reside permanently, and we'll stay with her whenever we come over, or rather whenever I come over. Sidney loves Bequia too much to live anywhere else. This house would suit a growing family, and I'm hoping to find occupants soon." She looked at the three adults, who were all smiling.

"Veronica never said she was moving to Dorsetshire Hill," said Rhoda.

"I told her ages ago I was building a couple of houses. However, when I put it to her, she said she was happy to move back to Dorsetshire Hill. The new house is sandwiched between two family homes, and Auntie's happy to live there; after all, she was born up there, and she accepted the Kingstown house is too large for one person. I guarantee she won't be lonely in her new home." Arlene sounded like someone whose plans were universally loved and therefore made her popular.

Veronica suffered crippling loneliness since her sister's death and welcomed regular visitors such as Rhoda with an enthusiasm she never showed before when Beryl was alive. Moving so far away would mean the visits would dry up; most of her visitors had no means of transport. Rhoda thought the move was a mistake for the elderly lady and that it may hasten her demise.

"But Veronica loves the town; she'd sit by the window watching the world pass by. And what about her visitors like me, who keep her company every week? She looks forward to that; she told me so." Rhoda was concerned for poor old Veronica.

"Dorsetshire Hill isn't that far away, and she was quite happy to move. If she had objected, I wouldn't have insisted. She'd be inundated with family up there, and she said she's looking forward to the move," said Arlene.

Rhoda didn't say anything else, but she wasn't convinced that Veronica would move from her decades-long home without any objections. She knew the old girl loved living in Kingstown; she had said so many times. She suspected that Arlene wanted to sell the old family home because she found no joy in visiting it since her mother's death and subsequently decided that it was too large for one person to live in. Rhoda was sure she had put heavily disguised pressure on Veronica to return to Dorsetshire Hill, her childhood home.

Verna found it all too much and said with a little impatience, "So who's going to live in this spacious house then?"

"You! If you want to!" Arlene had a broad smile from ear to ear displayed on her lightly lined, tanned face.

The visitors looked at each other baffled, then Herman burst out laughing, followed by howls from Verna and Rhoda.

"You're funny, Arlene. I know I got a promotion at work, Verna's doing OK at work, and we're buying our own little house. This one's too big and would be too much money to fork out monthly for rent or mortgage. Thanks, but no thanks!" Herman thought Arlene had lost a screw.

Verna said through laughter, "You're such a tease, Arlene; this is not us!"

Rhoda stopped laughing when she saw the smile evaporate from Arlene's face. She turned to the young people and gave them an angry stare.

"What's the matter, Ma, are you feeling OK?" asked Verna.

"Nothing's wrong with me; it's her!" Indicating Arlene with a sideways nod of her head.

Verna still didn't get it; she and Herman looked quizzically at Arlene, and it was he who caught on first. He became incensed that Arlene had planned their future without consulting them. He calmly said to her, "Thank you for your kindness, Arlene, but we'll not live in a house we couldn't afford. We'll finance our own when the time's right!"

Arlene tried to explain that she wasn't giving charity but hoped they'd be able to save up faster while living for free in her house. She miscalculated their reaction, thinking they'd see the house, be hooked and happily accept her offer. But she was thrown by the young couple's rejection.

When they returned home chastened after the surprises of that day, Verna's mind was a whirl of confusion. She and Herman couldn't stop talking about the day's events right into the night, which disturbed their sleep considerably. A coolness pervaded thereafter between Arlene and the people she called her 'other' family.

However, frail, lonely Veronica was soon dispatched to Dorsetshire Hill, and Rhoda seldom saw her thereafter. At first she saw her on a Sunday afternoon once a month when Herman had time to take her up there, but over time the visits became rarer. Rhoda had a way with words and presence when engaging with the elderly, and they never wanted her to leave after a visit, so it was with Veronica who would walk to the car with her when Herman came back to collect her. There were times tears clouded Veronica's pale blue eyes, and it didn't take a genius to see she was lonely and neglected; however, she put on an act for her neighbouring relatives and most of all, Arlene. Rhoda was powerless to help her, and it weighed heavily on her mind.

Veronica's old servants, Marlene, Hermie and the yardmen, were laid off and left to fend for themselves, though they all were given a small redundancy payment by a culpable Arlene. Some of her neighbouring relatives were very attentive, and she had a live-in maid to care for all her needs, but she still preferred Kingstown to the high, windy, though picturesque, Dorchester Hill.

Conclusion

It was a party to remember. Everyone was there: Arlene, Hermie and her family, Earl and his family, Lorna and hers, Ruby and almost all the others at Verna's office with their families; Herman's mother and aunt; his uncle had already passed away; and quite a number of friends and acquaintances gathered over the years. They all came to eat, drink, dance and indulge in loud West Indian camaraderie. That Saturday was filled with joy even though the morning rain was hard and steady, but it didn't dampen the spirits or expectations of the hosts or their guests. By early afternoon, when the party got started, the rain had stopped and was forgotton; the sky was all blue with not a wisp of white, the sun made skin searingly hot, and the ground was as dry as a bone; it was as though the rain had somehow magically never touched it.

The smiles of the couple were real, for they had come a long way in struggle and were glad they did it all themselves. Rhoda was busy with her centrepiece, a wonderfully large white iced cake trimmed with pink flowers, while the retired Hermie, full of grey hair but as strong as a woman half her age, and Leila, a salesperson at one of the town's larger stores, rushed around handing out drinks and making sure everyone was well catered to.

At around four o'clock, Earl turned the record player off, interrupting The Mighty Sparrow in his sweet calypsonian diatribe. Some of the guests were singing and dancing while others swung their hips and bodies, and even the smallest child was twisting, reeling, jerking and swaying to the wild melodic beat. He called for hush, which the adults did, but the children ignored and continued with their screeching, screaming and mad running inside and outside the house.

"Today," he boomed about the chaos, "we come here to celebrate Verna and Herman in more ways than one. Firstly, congratulations to Estelle, who won a scholarship to start high school education next term—"

He was interrupted with loud cheers, and the embarrassed child stood close to her mother with eyes downcast; she didn't want that and struggled to keep tears from flowing.

"—as ah was saying," he continued, "congrats to Estelle,

how fast she grow up. But we also here to wish her parents, my good friends Herman and Verna, a happy wedding anniversary and fourteen wonderful years. Raise yuh glasses to Herman and Verna and to this wonderful newly built house."

Glasses and small bottles were raised, everyone cheered louder and the cake was wheeled in. The couple cut the cake together, placed a piece in each other's mouth, to howls of laughter from the gathering, then they thanked everyone for coming to their celebration.

Herman then said, "I said to Verna, when we build our own house, we'll have a party, and here it is."

He looked at Verna, whose eyes were brimming over with emotion, remembering the many years of hard work and sometimes hardship they endured to get to where they were. They were overjoyed to be on Cane Garden Hill in a house they built that faced the blue sea with the smaller Grenadine islands and islets strung out in front of them.

Gradually, and as the twilight arrived unannounced, the party slid to a conclusion. The house became emptier and quieter till only Hermie and her family and Earl and his were left. Rhoda filled a basket with leftover food for Hermie, not out of pity but because there was so much left over and it would go to waste if not eaten in at least a day.

Leila was able to achieve the kind of job Verna had once craved, and she managed to improve her family's lot considerably. After she had her second child, she shook off the feeling of desperation she had entered, smartened herself up, and, to her surprise, acquired a job for a while in a small general store, eventually moving onto the largest store in town. By the time she and her family were guests at Verna and Herman's party, she was a floor supervisor; her retired mother kept house and looked after her children while she worked diligently. She and her family eventually moved out of Paul's Lot to Kingstown Park, a much better place a little further up the road.

The grey-haired, courteous and gentlemanly Earl also received a stuffed basket of goodies, which he and Hannah graciously accepted. Over the years he had grown from strength to strength, his business continuing to succeed, and he became so affluent that he and his family moved into a large house he had built just outside Layou beside the main road to Barrouallie, and some remarked as they passed by, 'that's Slim's house'. When his older son had to go to Grammar School in town, he was taken there every day by car. Soon Earl got fed up with people begging him to give their children lifts to school in town; most days the car was so full that Joel said it was dangerous and encouraged his boss to refuse the free loaders.

He tried to find ways to solve the problem without upsetting his customers, neighbours and friends. Then he had an inspired idea: he would purchase a bus to cater only for schoolchildren, he told Joel of his plan, who told him that he heard of a man in Chauncey who had a defunct bus with a good workable engine, which he had given up using. He and Joel went to see the bus owner, viewed the vehicle and he bought it there and then. He had the body rebuilt, the long wooden seats padded and the doors fitted for safety, then started his school bus service to the joy of many parents around the area.

Joel, who married Netty and was himself a father, volunteered to drive the bus, which was gladly accepted. Earl had buried his fear of driving, and with Joel's help, became a competent driver. He drove on the hair-raising Leeward roads with absolute confidence. Joel and Netty lived in Earl's old home upstairs over the store, he continued with barber work, but he no longer chauffeured his boss around.

Earl's fortune had also increased when his good friend Rudolf, Pearl's cousin, died and left him a bit of land large enough to accommodate a small house deep within the wilds of Largo Height. At first, not sure what to do with this legacy within an inhospitable terrain, he decided to sell it to someone willing to either build a house so far inland without proper roads or simply to use it to grow food. Trinidadian Julian, Rudolf's nephew and heir, didn't want the family land shared with strangers, so he suggested that Earl sell the plot back to him, which he gladly did.

Earl's sons were very bright, and the first boy, Everett, had won a scholarship to Grammar School, while he paid for his younger son, Eric, to go to the same school when he passed the entrance. He was overjoyed that his boys were academic and achieved the sort of education he could only dream of in his youth. For their sake, he tried hard to improve his diction; he didn't want to embarrass them in front of their friends. He noticed how Everett winced whenever he enunciated words badly. He would do anything for his sons but would never tolerate bad behaviour; his contemporaries often remarked that they were the best-behaved children in Layou.

The sun lay half-hidden on the horizon, and with the twilight furtively creeping in an almost eerie quiet pervaded all around. Verna stood on the driveway in front of their car, admiring the scenic maritime views in front of her. To her left, St Vincent's east coast snaked away, fading into the darkness. To her right lay Kingstown and its lush hills becoming mountainous cathedrals with spires pointing to the sky. In front of her, the Grenadines lay like sleeping children one would want to tiptoe around.

Someone came to her side and slipped their arm around her

waist. She turned and smiled, slipping her arm around their waist.

"You were right, you did it your way; you've your own house paid for by your own sweat and toil. I'm proud of you."

"Thank you, but I did say we'd do it ourselves sooner or later. I love it, not as big as yours, but it serves us well," she said quietly, dreamily.

"The past decade has seen quite a few changes for all of us. Veronica passed, Sidney gone so suddenly… I miss him; he was a good husband and friend. I was really lucky."

"Yeh, it was a shock hearing he passed away so suddenly, anyway, I'm glad you're back here for good. We did part on a sour note once, but things are well now, aren't they?" She gave Arlene a little squeeze.

"Of course, I'm sorry I upset you with the house and all that, but I wanted to give you something; I always wanted to give you something worthwhile."

"I always suspected that, but I have a mother, a good one at that. I've appreciated all you did for me, like encouraging me to read all those years ago."

"Do you feel fulfilled now or are you hankering for more?"

"Oh, don't tease, Arlene. I feel quite content with what I've got and with all the people I love around me. All my dreams came true, from the poor little semi-educated girl on Mayron to the sophisticated person I became. I don't want it to end." She gave a little nervous laugh.

"And why should it? You worked hard for everything you achieved, and you should be proud. From the moment I saw you all those years ago, I felt, bizarrely, you're the daughter I never had."

"I felt something too, but I thought it was my imagination. After we came from very different worlds, I never dreamt of anything like this," said Verna wistfully.

"Hey, you two," called Rhoda, interrupting the reverie, "come and help finish up this food!"

They walked back, arms entwined, to a quiet house and protested that they couldn't eat another thing while tucking into cake.

They all sat in the gallery, washing down the cake with coffee for some and mauby for others, and taking in the Kingstown scenery beneath them. The capital shone brightly with its many street lights competing with the bright moonlight. Verna's eyes narrowed as she tried to find her old home at New Montrose in the darkness. She was filled with love for her family, and as they rose to get ready for bed, she kissed each in turn. She accompanied Arlene to her home next door; they embraced, and with a kiss planted lovingly on her soft white cheek, she said, 'Goodnight, sleep tight' before returning home.

From her bed, Rhoda could see the Grenadines, and she wondered how her life would have been if she and her child had never left Mayron. In the room next door, her granddaughter slept soundly in her new bed in the new home, and further along the corridor, her daughter and her husband slept peacefully. Herman, snoring gently with the contented sleep of a successful man, while Verna dreamt sweet dreams of her life that turned out better than she had ever envisaged. All that she ever wanted came through: stable employment, a husband, a child and best of all, her own home.

"I love it here, so much better than New Montrose," said Estelle when the whole family, including Arlene, were eating Sunday lunch together some weeks later. "I love the close proximity to the sea and the Grenadines."

"I know what you mean, but we did see the sea and a few of

the Grenadines from New Montrose," added Rhoda.

"Only Bequia clearly," said Verna, "but here we can also see Battowia and Baliceaux; I find it relaxing."

"Could we go to Mayron again next school hols? I like it there, so small, so perfect!" said Estelle, remembering the first time she visited her mother's home island.

Her mother and grandmother looked at each other smiling as they remembered the old days – the hardships, the amity of the islanders, and the friends they left behind. They had no regrets leaving their home island and were happy it worked out admirably.

"Yes, we'd visit the little place, we'd call on people we once lived with, we'd visit family and friends in the cemetery, we'd lie on the pristine silver sand beaches, swim in the warm calm sea, and then we'd come back full of happy memories. Would that suit you, my beautiful daughter?" asked Verna, stretching her hand and cupping Estelle's.

"Indeed, that'll suit me very well," she beamed at the proud adults smiling sweetly at her, then continued eating.

"Amen!" proclaimed Herman.